A STONE STREWN CLASH

Forgotten Gods: Book Two

LEAH R CUTTER

Knotted Road Press

A Stone Strewn Clash
Forgotten Gods: Book Two
Copyright © 2020 Leah Cutter
All rights reserved
Published by Knotted Road Press
www.KnottedRoadPress.com

ISBN: 978-1-64470-136-2

Cover Art:

ID 104486331 © Sdecoret | Dreamstime.com
ID 144176144 © Archon7th | Dreamstime.com

Cover and interior design copyright © 2020 Knotted Road Press

http://www.KnottedRoadPress.com

Come someplace new…
Are you a traveler? Do you enjoy exploring strange new worlds, new cultures, new people?

Journey into the various lands envisioned by Leah Cutter.

Sign up for my newsletter and I'll start you on your travels with a free copy of my book, *The Island Sampler.*

I will never spam you or use your email for nefarious purposes. You can also unsubscribe at any time.

http://www.LeahCutter.com/newsletter/

The Fairy-Bridge Troll

The Troll-Demon War

The Troll-Human War

The Troll-Troll War

The Shadow Wars Trilogy

The Raven and the Dancing Tiger

The Guardian Hound

War Among the Crocodiles

The Clockwork Fairy Kingdom

The Clockwork Fairy Kingdom

The Maker, the Teacher, and the Monster

The Dwarven Wars

The Chronicles of Franklin

Franklin Versus The Popcorn Thief

Franklin Versus The Soul Thief

Franklin Versus The Child Thief

Huli Intergalactic - Science/Space Fantasy

Origins

The Strawberry Girl

Contemporary Fantasy

Siren's Call

The Immortals' War

Chapter One

WIND

GAN OU SLEPT FITFULLY, despite her exhaustion. She found her mind going back over the flight the day before, running from the Bone People, narrowly avoiding those cursed nets of theirs. Watching her companions fall and be captured. Had they been killed? Sacrificed to some dark god? Their flesh stripped away from their bones?

The guilt of having gotten away ate at her. She should have stayed to fight, to try to free her people. She couldn't call them friends, with the possible exception of Ka Lem, that serious young man who'd started all this trouble.

When Gan Ou did sleep, she had nightmares of being captured. A giant hand plucked her from the air and threw her down. The ground had disappeared from beneath her, and instead, she fell forever into a dark abyss that she couldn't escape from. Her heart froze and she struggled to move her limbs. She still tried, fighting to dance for Sune Li even while falling, to better carry her prayers to the god of the Wind People.

When the hard, cold dawn arrived, Gan Ou felt sick to her stomach, nausea sweeping over her, her gut in knots.

She still forced herself up to sitting, folding her legs under her and pulling her still warm blankets up over her shoulders. For a moment, she wished she had a cushion for her butt against the hard ground. Then she snorted at herself. There was never any point in wishing for things to be other than they were. She'd tried to break herself of that habit long ago, during her banishment from the lands of the Wind People, when she'd been forced to live among the rocks and hard places of the Stone People.

Seemed like she could still be as silly as she'd been as a youth. Or maybe this desire for wishing was because her banishment had finally been ended, and she could breathe the air of her homeland freely once again.

In the faint dawn light, she could just make out the others sleeping around her—three other Wind People, curled up in their blankets, along with two of the Stone People who slept, well, as still as piles of rocks.

The sun was still behind the thick forest to the east of the camp, dim and wan, barely bringing any light. She heard a river burbling to itself in the distance, somewhere behind her, trying to carry joy through the still morning. Clumps of snow lurked at the edges of the clearing, under the shadows of the trees, banished there by the weak sun but threatening to multiply and blanket the dried grass. The scent of smoke still coursed through the air, carried on the wind. Gan Ou tried to find a hint of the pines underneath it, but failed.

After a few deep breathes, Gan Ou closed her eyes and silently started her prayers, asking Sune Li for his blessing, his warmth, and his light. The words tasted like ashes, her guilt overwhelming. She doggedly continued, too stubborn to quit. The gods had never listened to her prayers before. That wasn't about to stop her from trying.

When Gan Ou finished her prayers, she found that the others had risen. Someone had started a fire, probably one of the youngsters. Two of the three other Wind People would be leaving soon, flying as fast as they could to the start of the messenger line, so the primary elders in the capital could be warned about the Bone People.

All of the Wind People needed to know that an army had gathered behind the wall of smoke, ready to invade their lands.

Both of the Stone People who had found their camp the night before had volunteered to go with Gan Ou, back through the great wall to face the Bone People. She'd grudgingly accepted their help, though that set the number of people in the rescue group to four. The luckiest number was three for all the People.

But she hadn't been able to talk the other Wind Person, Zhan Li, into staying behind, guarding the long cart that had brought the Stone People, or even traveling with the others back to the capital. And she had no authority to order him to do so either.

It did amuse Gan Ou that the Bone People had never encountered a stone person before. What would they think of the Sea People? They didn't even have hair!

Gan Ou stirred her old bones, stretching her arms up above her head as she stood. Damn it! This was a job for a youngster, not for someone in her sixties. She hurt in too many spots. The first time she'd tried escaping from the wall of smoke it had grabbed at her, pulling fur from her wolf body, which had turned into great gouges in her flesh as a person. Those areas still hadn't fully healed.

However, she couldn't leave the others behind, the ones who'd been captured by the Bone People. She'd already earned her freedom, and her banishment had been ended. Despite that, she still felt the need to prove herself, show that she was a worthy Wind Person. That she honored her people and her newly returned home.

She suspected that that stubbornness was going to get her killed one day.

———

GAN OU, Zhan Li, and the two Stone People, Noalanon and Daleki, came up with a simple plan to try to free the Wind and Stone People who'd been captured, at least in the closest camp of the Bone People. Basically, go in after dark, find the first camp, free all those they could find, then run away.

There was a good chance that not all the prisoners would be kept in the same place. They would quite probably be spread up and down the line of the wall, as originally, the Wind People had broken themselves up into several smaller groups and had passed through the wall in different places. Gan Ou and her team might end up having to rescue more than one collection of prisoners, though they wouldn't try to free them all in a single night.

First, though, they had to wait until nightfall. While all the people could see fairly well in the dark, the Stone People could see the best, particularly if they were underground or in caves, surrounded by rock.

Chances were, the Bone People wouldn't be able to see as well as the Stone People at night. Even if there had been a full moon (which it wasn't) the light from the stars would be blocked by the smoke and haze that still filled the air.

Gan Ou hated waiting. She was used to it—she felt as though she'd been waiting for most of her life. She tried to sleep, and managed for a while, out from under the trees in the wan sunlight. When she woke, she found Noalanon standing nearby, zir face turned upwards, toward the sun, like some sort of flower.

Noalanon turned to smile at Gan Ou when she sat up.

"The sun feels so cold here," ze said, though ze remained smiling. "The stones though, are solid and warm."

Only then did Gan Ou glance down and realize that Noalanon stood barefoot on a long pale rock that barely stuck up above the dried grass and earth.

"The sun should be warmer," Gan Ou said, glaring skyward. "Too much damned smoke is in the way." The sun looked like a tiny orange ball, its brightness so dimmed that she could gaze directly on it.

That was just wrong.

Noalanon nodded and stayed quiet while Gan Ou rolled up her sleeping blankets and pillow into a tight bundle. When she finished, she realized the Stone Person was watching her, an expectant look on the teacher's face.

"Out with it," Gan Ou said. She tried to modulate her tones to be less gruff, though she doubted she succeeded. Fortunately, Noalanon had known Gan Ou for years and wasn't likely to take offense easily.

"When you first went through the wall, you thought you found a missing space inside of yourself, where magic might belong," Noalanon said slowly.

Gan Ou gave zir a sharp nod. "Aye. I knew, somehow, that there is a spell that would blow the wall away. Or a dance, maybe." She shrugged. "Don't know what that spell is, though. Or how to find it. Didn't feel as though I *could* find it. It felt…it felt as though I needed to be taught. That I needed someone to show me." Gan Ou shook her head, frustrated.

"Who would know such a spell?" Noalanon asked.

Gan Ou knew that Noalanon tried to keep zir voice soothing, but the question still irritated her. "If I knew that, I would have already gone to see them," she snapped. "The knowledge is…lost."

"In the archives, the Stone People have many books,"

Noalanon said. "Like that book, from olden times, that contained the pictures of horses."

Gan Ou nodded. She'd tried to find the form of the horse. It had been very difficult for her, much more difficult than it had been for the other Wind People around her. Was that just because she was old? Or was it because her feet were still unused to standing in the lands of her people?

She'd never told anyone how much harder it had become to find any of the forms, the longer she stood in the lands of the Stone People.

"Do you think that maybe the spell was written down? That it could somehow be learned from a book?" Noalanon said.

"No," Gan Ou said immediately. "It's more of a feeling than a picture." She paused, considering her words. "Think of it this way. It's difficult to describe the feeling that one of your beautiful stone statues can give. Particularly one that stands in a courtyard lit by the sunlight. How the shadows play across it, the way the stone subtly changes color. You have to see it. That's what this hole feels like. I know I could do that spell. I just have to see it, feel it, once."

Noalanon nodded slowly. "Do you have any stories about people able to call up great winds?"

Gan Ou felt herself smile. It was still an expression that seemed vaguely foreign to her. "I thought of that, and went to ask one of the older storyteller in the capital about it. He told me the story of Ru An, one of the minor heroes, who had control over the winds and used them to blow out all the campfires of her enemy."

"That would be a useful trick," Noalanon said. Ze paused, thinking for a moment. "We have a myth about being able to 'waken' stones, so that they'll keep track of any who pass."

"All right..." Gan Ou said. She wasn't certain where

Noalanon was going with this.

"I've been spending the day trying to put more feeling into the rocks in the area," Noalanon said. "So that if I get lost, I'd be able to find my way here again."

"Any luck?" Gan Ou asked, curious.

"None," Noalanon said with a grimace. "Like you, I think I need to be shown the first time. Then I'd be able to do it."

Gan Ou looked at the slab of stone that Noalanon still stood on. Zir toes stretched and flexed, unconsciously, as if trying to dig their way through, to find better ground underneath.

"Is it more difficult here in the land of the Wind People? Than it was in your lands?" Gan Ou said.

At Noalanon's confused expression, Gan Ou tried to explain. "Does the land here support you? Or is it harder?"

"It's more difficult here," Noalanon said quietly. "I can't explain it. The ground doesn't fight me. But it doesn't support me either. Not like the lands of the Stone People."

"I felt that as well," Gan Ou said. "I think many do." She paused, then asked, "Are you having difficulty 'waking' a rock because it's here? In the lands of the Wind People? Or do you think you might be able to do it better in your own lands?"

Noalanon shrugged. "I don't know if I could just waken a rock in the land of the Stone People either."

"Let's try," Gan Ou said, picking up her sleeping roll and heading back to the cart that had made the journey all the way from the lands of the Stone People.

The back of the cart was piled high with many goods: sleeping rolls for both the Wind and Stone People, jerked meat, dried fruit and nuts, as well as the minerals that the Stone People needed. Unlike the Sea and the Wind People, the Stone People couldn't survive on the food of the other people. Without their special minerals, they'd starve.

Gan Ou wasn't certain exactly what starving would look like for a Stone Person. Would they shrink down, like a mountain of sand pummeled by rain? Or would they freeze up, and slowly turn into a pile of rocks?

The minerals were contained in a wooden trunk that was reinforced with metal on the outside. It was lined with waxed leather on the inside, to make it more waterproof. A dozen highly polished stone boxes sat inside the trunk, each about six inches square, as well as six inches deep, all of them sealed tightly with waxy membranes around the lids.

Each box contained a different mineral that the Stone People needed for their sustenance. They would pick and choose, depending on how they felt, eating perhaps only three or four different minerals per day, but needing all twelve over a week's time. The boxes were made from different types of rock: granite, marble, agate, flint, and others that Gan Ou couldn't name. They were certainly pretty, and ranged in color from alabaster to ebony, with blues, greens, ambers, and purples in between.

"Could you 'waken' one of these?" Gan Ou asked, opening the trunk and pointing to the stone containers inside of it.

Noalanon looked carefully at the boxes. "I'm not sure," ze said slowly. "I'm afraid to try, actually. Afraid that I'll spoil the minerals somehow by 'waking' them."

Gan Ou nodded. That made sense to her. Though her people ate fresh vegetables, they rarely ate raw meat, and certainly not something that was still living.

"How about we scoop out the minerals from one of the containers, put them in something else, and then you can try? Gan Ou proposed.

Noalanon still looked uncertain, but after a few more moments of consideration, ze nodded.

"That one," ze said, pointing to a gray box. The color of

the stone practically matched the color of Noalanon's skin. Gan Ou wasn't sure what it was, maybe a type of soft limestone.

Daleki and Zhan Li came over to watch. They listened quietly to Noalanon's explanation while Gan Ou got one of the empty water skins of the Wind People and poured the minerals into it. She had no idea what the mineral was, and knew that she wouldn't understand the description even if she asked for it. It was coarsely ground, black with flecks of light brown. It was also slightly moist, which surprised her. She'd always thought that all the minerals the Stone People consumed needed to be completely dry.

When Gan Ou finished emptying the container, Noalanon asked her to put the open stone box on the edge of the cart.

Gan Ou and the others took a step back while Noalanon stepped forward. The Stone Person put zir hands on either side of the stone box, then closed zir eyes and concentrated.

Gan Ou watched the Stone Person's hands. Would she be able to see anything?

Light suddenly shot out from between Noalanon's fingers, causing Gan Ou and the others to take another quick step backwards.

What did that mean? Had Noalanon been successful?

The light faded, and the box went back to being a normal gray stone again.

Noalanon dropped zir hands and stepped away from the edge of the cart. Zir head hung down. Gan Ou could tell the Stone Person was exhausted, just from the way Noalanon held zirself.

"I think…I think it's done," Noalanon said. Zir voice sounded hoarse, like rocks grinding together.

"Good for you!" Gan Ou said firmly, though a part of her was shaken.

Ka Lem had said that they were all entering the time when they'd find out if the legends were true. He may have been right.

Noalanon took a deep breath and raised zir head. Ze blinked. "I know where that stone sits, now." Ze turned zir back. "Even when I can't see it."

"Hopefully, that means that if we get separated, you'll be able to find your way back here," Gan Ou said. "Or even make it through the magical wall with fewer difficulties."

Noalanon nodded zir head.

"Go. Sleep. Now," Gan Ou said. "Or you'll be useless to us later."

That earned her a sly smile. "Yes, Mana," Noalanon said, using the Stone People's word for the one who carried a child.

While Gan Ou got Noalanon settled down on blankets, Zhan Li and Daleki tried the experiment again. However, Daleki couldn't 'waken' any of the stone boxes. Ze didn't feel drawn to any of them, not like Noalanon had. And ze didn't feel drawn to the one that Noalanon had woken either.

That worried Gan Ou. It meant that Daleki was much more vulnerable. Plus, ze was going to be less likely to press on if they were attacked.

There wasn't anything she could do about it, however. Except wait, sitting beside Noalanon, keeping guard over the pile of rocks that would eventually waken and join them again.

THE NIGHT FELT THICKER than usual, the darkness all encompassing. Gan Ou wasn't sure if it was because of the overwhelming smoke, or if it was something else, some other deviltry in the air, put there by the Bone People.

Winter pressed in harder on them as well. It would snow before dawn. Gan Ou shivered next to their campfire, sipping at the hot stew she and Zhan Li shared for dinner. The Stone People had cups carved out of rock that they'd brought with them from their home. They warmed the stone, as well as the liquid inside the cups with their own hands. It was a useful trick. Gan Ou had enjoyed more than one cup of tea from water warmed that way when she'd been living in the Stone People's capital.

The group didn't talk much. They had their plan. They had their fears to overcome. They had their people to go and rescue.

Finally, when the night had grown solid and Gan Ou felt herself starting to slow down as it was approaching the time she normally went to sleep, the group killed the fire and started off. Gan Ou led the way. She couldn't say why she knew exactly which direction the wall ran, but she did. She could feel it in a way that made her deeply uncomfortable. It was like knowing that a stain clung to your favorite coat, one that you could never just brush away.

She stopped a few feet from the cool misty wall. Without comment, she stripped off the robe she wore and transformed into a powerful ram, with curling horns and strong hind quarters. She'd be able to run quickly, as well as headbutt anyone who tried to stop her.

Zhan Li transformed into a large brown bear, with sharp claws and wicked teeth. His eyesight wouldn't be as good as hers, particularly in the fog and smoke. And he also couldn't run as fast as she could. But he would be able to defend himself better.

Their biggest concern was the magical nets of the Bone People. They were weighted, and would cause a Wind Person to fall down and pass out. They would also drain the magic from a Wind Person. Gan Ou had seen a pony transform into a Wind Person under such a net, though the person was unconscious.

Both Noalanon and Daleki were armed with sharp obsidian knives that they hoped would cut through the nets. Once the group passed through the wall, the two Stone People would harden their skin so that arrows and steel knives wouldn't hurt them. Plus, they could burn up any net thrown over their head, and possibly protect the Wind People.

Gan Ou led them through the wall, pushing herself forward, fighting the ram's instincts to run away. The coldness didn't strike her as hard as it had the other two times she'd gone through the wall. Either she was getting used to it, or this animal form didn't feel the cold or magic as acutely as a wolf did.

The ground under the ram's hooves lost its solid feel midway through, and instead, it felt as though she was pushing through thick grass. The smell of smoke overwhelmed all her other senses. Gan Ou was obstinate. It took her longer than it had the first time, the wall thicker than it had been. Or maybe it just felt that way, walking through pitch blackness through the cold and wet.

Finally, Gan Ou reached the other side, feeling, more than hearing, a soft *pop*. She took a few steps to the side and stood completely still, hoping to avoid any guards who might be nearby.

The Stone People came out next, followed by Zhan Li. Noalanon and Daleki took a few moments to harden their skin, then they started leading the way.

Gan Ou took a deep breath and told herself to be patient. She'd known that the Stone People, particularly after they'd hardened their skin, would move more slowly. Maybe that was why Zhan Li had chosen the form of a bear—he'd be happier ambling along than the quick footed ram.

Though Gan Ou couldn't see anything in the thick darkness, Noalanon led them straight across the rutted plane. Finally, a spark of light appeared in the distance, and grew as they approached.

The Bone People's campfire.

Gan Ou's heart started beating more rapidly. She had to push down on the instincts of the ram, who wanted to paw the ground and snort, then race full on into the camp, butting and kicking and doing as much damage as it could.

Noalanon leaned over and whispered in Gan Ou's ear, "Wait here." Then the Stone Person moved off. Gan Ou quickly lost sight of zir. A few feet away, she heard the shuffling of the bear, could smell it dusty fur.

She couldn't make herself lie down on the cold ground, as much as she wanted to. However, it was almost impossible to stay still. She picked up her feet, constantly moving from side to side, or turning in small circles. The night grew tense. Her nerves sang at a high-pitched tone in her head. Dust and ash covered her mouth and dulled her sense of smell.

Oh, she longed to run forward. Could already feel the dried winter grass pounding beneath her hooves. The bony ridge of her forehead would easily throw any opposition to the ground. Then she could stomp on them, kick them away.

Wait.

Gan Ou grew completely still. Who had said that? It wasn't one of the Stone People. Nor had it been Zhan Li. But she had no doubt that she'd heard the word, that it had been carried on the wind specifically to her ear.

After an immeasurable time, Gan Ou watched two shadows drawing near, eventually resolving into Noalanon and Daleki.

Noalani bent over slightly and whispered in Gan Ou's ear.

"The Wind People are being kept on the far side of the

camp. They are chained together at the ankles with a magical chain that prevents them from taking other forms. The dead elk…"

The voice paused. Gan Ou sensed Noalanon give a deep shudder, as if overcoming zir revulsion.

"The dead elk are there, close to the prisoners at the far side of the camp. We believe that they will raise an alarm when we begin to free people. They tracked us, watched us, though the guards never saw us."

Gan Ou nodded to indicate that she understood.

How were they going to break the magical chain? If it were easy to escape from, surely the Wind People would have already freed themselves.

While Gan Ou didn't think that any of the People would do well in captivity, she knew that it would grind down the Wind People most of all.

However, she couldn't ask about the chain or the plan, didn't have a mouth that could form questions. Instead, she followed along after Noalanon, growing completely still whenever the Stone Person did, and a guard passed by without seeing them.

Gan Ou was glad she was in ram form when she saw the thick chains tied to the ankles of the Wind People. If she'd been a bear like Zhan Li, she didn't know if she'd have been able to prevent herself from growling.

Even in the dim light thrown from the fire in the center of the camp, she could tell that the shackles had damaged the Wind People. Their skin was covered in sores and scabs from where the metal rubbed against it.

She didn't see any easy way to remove the shackles, no pin or hinges. How had the Bone People put them on? Did they meld metal the same way that the Sea People melded glass, or the Stone People worked with rock?

Her people were good with wood, as well as all living

things, but they didn't have a particular material that they worked with.

A fleeting image came to her, of leaves swirling around her. Before she could pursue the thought, she saw the dead elk.

The bucks looked so wrong, their antlers put on their bare skulls backwards, making them constantly dip their heads as the weight pushed at them awkwardly. Their bones shone with a sickly blue glow. A chain was wrapped around their necks, holding them in place. They barely moved their feet, and only occasionally shuffled back and forth. It was unnatural.

Their eyes were the worst, though. Burning with a fire that seared Gan Ou's hide.

What would it feel like to headbutt one of them? Would the antlers just break off? Or would they stab at Gan Ou, burn her flesh?

Before she could find out, Noalanon touched her front leg, drawing her attention back to the line of Wind People chained before them. The prisoners all stayed lying on the ground, trying not to draw attention to themselves. The chain looped between the shackles on their legs, connecting them to each other. The far end of the chain was staked to the ground, held down with a huge block of iron that Gan Ou doubted even a Stone Person would be able to easily pick up and move.

Noalanon reached down and wrapped zir hand around the chain leading from the Wind Person on the end—someone Gan Ou didn't know—to the block.

Gan Ou watched, fascinated, as the iron grew red hot, shining against the skin of the Stone Person. However, Noalanon couldn't get the iron hot enough for it to melt. Ze tried pulling on the links on either side of the two red ones, but ze wasn't strong enough to yank them apart.

Try cold.

Gan Ou's ears pricked up. Who was speaking? Where were those words coming from? Again, she felt as though they'd been carried on the wind, directly to her ears, and that no one else could hear them.

The same words had been brought to Noalanon, though. Ze dropped the chain, shook zir hands, and then grasped it again, a few links down, this time applying cold.

It wasn't as easy to see as the heat. The chain didn't start glowing, and it was too dim to see any ice crystals forming on the huge links.

However, after just a few long moments, Noalanon dropped the chain, then struck it with all zir might.

The links shattered with a loud cracking sound.

Gan Ou's head jerked up, looking all around. Damn it! Had the guards heard?

A similar crackling noise came from the distance, where Gan Ou assumed the other end of the chain had been broken.

A soft sigh came to her, carried on the breeze.

The chain no longer being attached to the mighty iron anchors appeared to have damaged the magic it carried. The Wind Person closest to Gan Ou slowly began to change form, her ankles thinning so that she could slip them out of the shackles as her wings sprouted. She leapt into the air, a large black-headed goose.

Shouts came now, angry voices. The guards were awake and coming for them.

Gan Ou wheeled and headbutted the first guard she found, tossing him onto his back with all the force she could muster. She heard loud growls and screeches around her in the dark.

When one of those damned nets landed across her back,

Gan Ou fell hard on her front knees, struggling. It wouldn't do for the rescuers to need rescuing!

However, Noalanon was suddenly beside her. Zir obsidian knife easily cut through the rope net. Gan Ou struggled to her feet, shaking her head, woozy.

They needed to leave. They'd freed their people. Tomorrow night they would repeat the process at a different camp.

Noalanon wrapped zir arms around Gan Ou's neck, pulling zirself slowly up onto Gan Ou's back, then clinging tightly. The Stone Person weighed so much! Gan Ou tried not to resent the pile of rocks she carried.

Gamely, Gan Ou started running. She knew exactly which direction the wall was in. She ran into two more guards, knocking them over in her haste to escape.

Another net was thrown over her. Gan Ou stumbled but kept trying to run.

Noalanon cut the net off before it stopped Gan Ou completely.

Then the wall was in front of her. Gan Ou hadn't thought she'd been running that fast. Maybe the wall had moved back toward the camp in order to protect the Bone People?

It didn't matter. She was plunging in through the cold, the mist blinding her as effectively as the dark night had done earlier.

The wall seemed thinner. She burst out on the other side, racing toward safety.

They'd done it! They'd freed the first group of prisoners!

She didn't allow herself to think about how many more times they'd have to go and do that. Or how much more difficult it would become as the Bone People learned their tricks.

Chapter Two

STONE

SUGAOSHI SAT IN ZIR OFFICE, distracted. Ze had being trying to focus on the reports in front of zir, on the lists of books created by or about the Wind People that the archivists had found among the stacks. However, the sunlight was too tempting. It made beautiful patterns on the black and white stone mosaic covering the floor of zir office. Ze longed to go outside and bask in the sunlight, just for a little while. Besides, it was winter. There wouldn't be that many beautiful days for the next few months.

Though it was cool outside, Sugaoshi could raise zir own internal temperature and never feel it. Plus, ze could also use a snack, a quick mouthful of the delicate minerals that were served close to the gate of the market. Something to put a zing in zir step.

Ze could just step outside for a few moments, breathe a little bit of fresh air before ze got back to zir work. Or maybe ze needed to take the day off, go back to zir latest painting…

Sugaoshi shook zir head. No, ze had work to do. Ze could paint later. Ze had promised to go see a play with zir friends that evening. However, they all understood that the art came first.

So resolved, Sugaoshi pushed zirself up. The Stone People didn't feel stiff, or have the aches and pains that the other People did. As they grew older, they would start moving more slowly. And they would lose strength as well. Though Sugaoshi was the youngest member of the council, and had just turned thirty, ze still felt zir age, quite possibly more than others.

Normally, a Stone Person lived until they were seventy or eighty. Zir Mana, however, had died in zir fifties, as had zir Grandmana.

Sugaoshi tried to make the most of every day as a result, particularly as ze aged.

So today, ze would go spend a little time out in the beautiful sunlight. Maybe take a stroll through the main city park. Then ze would buckle down and really start working again.

Sugaoshi had always found it odd that the Wind People didn't have parks. Then again, they barely had cities. They did have corridors of wilderness, trees and meadows, running through all of the main villages. As well as too many trees. That always struck Sugaoshi as just dirty.

At least the Sea People had fountains everywhere, even if it was merely so they could wash their feet regularly. Such an odd habit.

Juhala had found another teacher to work as the liaison between the other Peoples and the council. Ze had originally approached Sugaoshi about taking up the work.

That was *not* zir place, nor was it the purview of the artists who ze represented. No, teachers were the go between of the different Peoples. It was bad enough that ze had had to study them by going through the archives.

With a sigh, Sugaoshi stepped out of zir office and into

the bright winter day. The blue sky was prettier than any agate. No clouds marred the expanse, though chill winds still blew, teasing zir jacket and tugging at zir hair. Sugaoshi set zir temperature a bit warmer to combat the cold. Then ze walked through the small front yard, out the gate and onto the street.

Before recently, ze had never thought about how nice it was to have gravel sidewalks, as well as stone-covered streets, instead of always walking in dirt, like the Wind People. How could they live like that? More like the animals they could become than like real people.

Then again, they frequently became animals and walked down the streets instead of being civilized and using carts or carriages.

Sugaoshi determinedly turned zir thoughts back to the sunny day. The low wall separating the row of small offices from the street had been built out of field rock, nubbly and full of different browns, grays, and blacks. The way the sunlight struck it was always interesting, the surface creating different shadows throughout the day.

Just a few blocks away sat the main park. A white stone archway marked the entrance, wide enough for four people to pass abreast. Trails of different colored gravel led off the main gray walkway, inviting one to amble between the fountains and statues, or to sit for a while on one of the beautifully carved stone benches.

Sugaoshi breathed in the peaceful air of the park. To the side, a Stone {erson sat on a bench with three young ones playing around zir, their shrieks like loud birds. Two older people walked slowly toward Sugaoshi, their heads together, seriously discussing the state of the world.

Beauty lay all around Sugaoshi, filling zir heart with joy. This was what ze'd needed this morning. Not to stay in zir stuffy office, but to get outside, experience the world again.

Though Sugaoshi didn't want to admit it, ze knew that ze was having too many days like this, when ze pushed the work off, then had to scramble to get everything done. It might be time for zir to step down from office, to go back to just painting.

But ze had wanted to make a difference, to represent the artists in Killapany in a way that no one else had ever been able to. While some artists were like Sugaoshi, neat and clean, their offices and their studios sparse and uncluttered, most were like zir friend Valiana, who had every horizontal space covered with paint or brushes, canvases piled up in the corner in all stages (none of them complete) with very little to ever show after even several days of work.

It was just so tiresome, this news being carried from the Wind People's lands. Though ze had voted to send people to the Wind People's lands, to show support, it still rankled that they had needed it. Ze resented these stupid Bone People and the trouble they were causing.

Why had this happened during zir tenure?

Zir took a deep breath of the cool morning air. Though the situation didn't make zir happy, ze also knew that ze was one of the best artists to handle this affair. Ze could be disciplined. And ze would make a difference.

With zir back straight and zir head held high, Sugaoshi recommitted to being the best damned council member that ze could be during this crisis. Ze would work as hard as ze could, and bring as much skill and yes, art to whatever negotiations needed to go on.

Once it was all over, though, ze was going to retire. Maybe find a cottage outside the city where ze could spend zir days gazing at the holy mountain and painting all the aspects of it.

So resolved, Sugaoshi made zir way back to zir office,

with only a short stop for a warm spoonful of delicate minerals on the way.

***

SUGAOSHI SAT STUNNED with the rest of the council.

Over fifty of the Bone People approached the city! And several of the dead elk traveled with them!

The councilmembers had quickly gathered in an emergency session in the council chambers as soon as the news was brought to the city. Sugaoshi felt as though the polished marble walls reflected back their surprised, amplifying it. The solid granite desk the members sat behind felt good against zir hands as the rest of the world seemed to have shifted.

How had the Bone People gotten here so fast? Obviously, they hadn't all been waiting behind that wall of theirs. What did they want? Why were they here?

The first question of business quickly settled down into where should the council meet with them?

Mahletik, the oldest council member and the representative of the wealthy mine owners, wanted to meet the Bone People outside of the city. "Once we welcome them inside Killapany, we'd never be able to ask them to leave," ze growled. Ze wore the richest clothing of all of them, with a beautiful black vest embroidered with pure silver thread over an emerald green shirt. Sugaoshi felt the color combination was a bit dated, the contrast overdone.

Yagakilly, who represented the merchants, disagreed strongly. "We might offend them by forcing them to stay outside of the city," ze argued. "Think of the trade opportunities they may have to offer." At least ze wore a modern shirt, crimson in color with a nice sheen to it.

"And we need them to be closer, so that we can learn

about them. Study them," Juhala said. Ze represented the teachers, so of course ze wanted to learn about the foreign People. Ze was always so serious, as if being studious could make up for not being very bright. Ze was in zir customary black shirt with the high collar, which admittedly looked good against zir fine dark skin and set off zir pale gray eyes.

It surprised Sugaoshi when Kinrahsy, the representative of the builders, agreed. "Aye, we need them close. To watch and learn." Ze wore shades of brown today, the collar and cuffs contrasting with the rest of zir shirt. The combination was actually more interesting than Sugaoshi would have thought Kinrahsy was capable of.

The other councilmembers all turned to Sugaoshi, to get zir opinion. It didn't really matter what ze said. Three of the five councilmembers had already voted to allow the Bone People into the city. This was just stating zir opinion for the record.

"They will learn as much about us as we do about them, once we grant them access to the city," ze said slowly. That thought made zir shiver, as if a cold wind had just blown through the broad council chamber. Others, too, seemed to feel the same chill effect.

"I would bring them into the city," Sugaoshi said slowly, feeling zir way through the topic. "And assign them the heartiest, strongest Stone People for their guides. As well as the most magical. Lead the Bone People to believe that even the weakest of us are that capable."

The other councilmembers nodded in agreement. Of course, they wouldn't have thought of such things. They weren't artists. They didn't understand the theatricality of a good show, how useful illusions could be.

"I doubt we can hide any aspect of our lives," Sugaoshi added after a moment. "Like our need for minerals for subsistence. However, it might be useful for them to believe that we just 'eat dirt.' Do what we can to disguise, or reframe, anything that might be perceived of as a weakness."

"Yes," Mahletik said. Ze gave Sugaoshi a broad smile. "I vote that Sugaoshi come up with a list of our abilities to showcase, as well as those we want to deflect interest from."

Sugaoshi nearly groaned out loud. More work. Ze wasn't going to get back to zir painting tonight, that was for damned sure.

The members of the council all agreed to find at least half a dozen people from their various districts who could act as official tour guides to the Bone People in the city. That way, they could all take turns, and no one would have to bear the burden of the work.

Juhala looked relieved. Had ze actually believed that these tasks would all fall on the shoulders of the teachers? Of course ze had. Ze was too puffed up and thought too much of zirself and the importance of zir role.

They all had work ahead of them. Despite the huge tasks facing Sugaoshi, ze was actually looking forward to the challenge. Though ze wasn't great at making lists, the thought of the artifice ze was creating, crafting the face of the Stone People for the newcomers, was thrilling.

Perhaps this was what ze had been born to do, why ze needed to stay in the council.

A TALL BONE Person faced the councilmembers, standing apart from the rest of zir group in the council chamber, a dozen of them in all. The other Bone People looked around curiously at the marble mosaic that they stood on, done in white, black, and rust in the shape of a five-pointed star. The councilmember's desk rose up high in front of them, beautifully carved out of gray and black stone. The walls met with Sugaoshi's approval as well, made out of a polished white marble, creamy and shot through with gold.

Sugaoshi studied the strange new People in front of zir carefully. The Bone People weren't much taller than the Wind People, who were generally about five feet to five feet five in height. Which meant the Bone People were shorter than the Stone People, a thought that made Sugaoshi unrepentantly happy.

However, instead of being all the colors of wood like the Wind People—reds and browns and grays—the Bone People were much more pale, white with pink hues to their skin. At least as far as Sugaoshi could tell. The Bone People were completely covered up, from neck to wrists to ankles. Ze couldn't see any of the rest of their skin.

The clothing they wore was baggy as well, in colors of greens, browns, and grays. All the colors were muted, making the bright yellow of their hair stand out, along with the paleness of their skin.

The spokesperson for the Bone Person went by the curious name of Heimir. Sugaoshi would learn all of the traveler's names eventually, but ze concentrated on this Heimir at first. Zir baggy green shirt seemed roughly made, not refined. It probably felt coarse as well, though the dye job looked even. Ze wore a wide brown leather belt around zir waist, about the width of Sugaoshi's hand. Decorative patterns had been embossed along the edges. Were they just for decoration? Or did they indicate some sort of rank, as not all the members of the Bone People wore similar belts?

The pants were probably wool, and an ugly brown. The boots also seemed well made, dyed black and with solid soles.

Knives and weighted nets hung off the belts of many of the Bone People. Evidently, they'd been surprised to be allowed into the council chamber carrying their weapons. They had no idea that the knives wouldn't cut the skin of the

Stone People. In addition, their nets, while they might be heavy enough to bring down one of the Wind People probably wouldn't drag a Stone Person down. The Stone People were much, much stronger. Mere netting wouldn't stop them.

The Bone People appeared to feel the cold like the Wind People. Several of them wore fur vests and knit scarves, bundled up to keep themselves warm. They'd been suitably awed when one of their guides had warmed their room, not by something so crude as a fire but by heating the rocks of their hearth.

The council chamber had no such heating source, as visitors from the other People were infrequent. Everyone could just raise their own internal temperatures instead. Even elderly Stone People could do that much, at least.

Mahletik was the designated speaker that morning. Ze sat in the center of the rest of the councilmembers, directly in front of the Bone People, who Sugaoshi couldn't help but think of as supplicants. Ze wore the same black and silver embroidered vest, though this time ze'd matched it with a much more appropriate navy blue shirt. The buttons on the vest were made from pure silver, a little ostentatious, but Sugaoshi approved.

"Greetings," Mahletik said graciously, as if this were the first time ze had met with the Bone People. It was, in a way, as now they were all acting in their official capacities. "You have traveled far to reach our fair capital. We would know the reason for your journey." Ze left it at that. Let the Bone People come up with their own reasons for showing up.

"Trouble has reached our home, far to the east," Heimir said. "The fields no longer bear as many crops of wheat, rye, and other grains. We come searching for answers, as well as for possible trade. Maybe new fields as well."

Sugaoshi had no idea if ze lied. Ze had the most

experience with all artifice and disguises, and so should be best able to distinguish truth from fiction. However, ze hadn't had enough time to study the Bone People, to learn their tells. Yet.

If forced to make a guess, ze would say that there was some truth to Heimir's words. However, ze spoke only a partial truth. There were other forces at work, of that Sugaoshi had no doubt.

"Traveling all the way through the lands of the Wind People to reach us, the Stone People, seems an awfully long distance to come just for trade," Yagakilly stated. Ze was most familiar with merchants, and would be in charge of any bargains to be made. Ze wore another beautifully crafted shirt, a dark gray, the color of a deep mountain lake.

Heimir nodded. "That is not the only reason we have come," ze stated. "We also bring word of Valtyr to all the People."

Sugaoshi blinked. It wasn't a name that ze was familiar with. Then again, as far as ze knew, there were no myths about the Bone People, no stories or even rumors of them.

Because it appeared to be required, Mahletik asked, "And who is Valtyr?"

Heimir drew zirself up to zir full height.

Sugaoshi didn't want to point out to Heimir that zir head was still a good foot or so beneath the top of the desk that the councilmembers sat at. Standing up taller wouldn't bring zir anywhere close to looking at them directly.

"I am a priest of Valtyr," Heimir said. "You all know him, though you have forgotten his name. It is our duty to educate you about his great deeds and presence."

Sugaoshi blinked, surprised. Why would one of the Bone People care that their god be known by the other Peoples? Surely the Bone People had more than enough supplicants to offer prayers to this Valtyr.

"Valtyr came before any of your gods," Heimir said. "His home is the abyss, which your gods drew away from. But Valtyr was first."

Sugaoshi wasn't exactly sure why being first mattered. The Wind, Sea, and Stone People all believed their god had been born first and was the most important. Though ze had to admit that a god of the darkness, of the abyss that Kiproary had formed zirself out of, made sense.

Darkness appeared to flow from Heimir, a thick inky blackness that stretched out to the sides, touching the walls of the chamber, then flowing upward toward the councilmembers.

Sugaoshi instinctively knew that ze should never let that filth touch zir. It was worse than the dirt that filled the streets and houses of the Wind People. Regular earth ze would be able to wash off.

This would taint zir soul.

Ze didn't have time to run, however. Instead, ze spiked zir internal temperature upward, possibly high enough for zir own almost black skin to start glowing. The beautiful white jacket ze wore, one that ze had decorated with beautiful, hand-painted red poppies, started to smoke. Ze felt zir brown hair lift off zir shoulders from the wave of heat.

Then the darkness passed, dissipating as quickly as the morning fog that wreathed the holy mountain.

Sugaoshi expected Mahletik to start yelling, to get angry and abrasive at being attacked in their own council chambers.

However, the rich mine owner sat with zir face slack for a moment, working zir jaw before the words came grating out. "I see," ze said slowly.

Crap. Sugaoshi couldn't say for certain, but ze would bet that the mine owner had taken that blackness into zir soul.

Sugaoshi studied the other councilmembers closely.

Juhala also appeared unaffected. Surely ze hadn't been smart enough to burn off the abyss before it filled zir. Maybe ze had just been too stupid to corrupt. Yagakilly might also have escaped the effects.

But Kinrahsy had the same slack-jawed appearance as the mine owner. As they were the oldest councilmembers, the rest of the councile tended to defer to the pair.

Heimir and the contingent of Bone People all looked up smugly at the council. They'd obviously believed that their ruse had worked, that they now had some level of control over the council.

Sugaoshi wasn't about to alert them of their failure. "Dark and light," ze said after a moment. "It makes sense."

The other councilmembers all looked over at zir. "Don't you get it?" ze asked, putting as much disdain into zir voice as possible. "It's all about negative space. That which isn't there is as important as that which is." Ze looked over at Heimir. "As an artist, I understand at a deeper level than the others."

It was all a lie. However, the Bone People had no idea what were the tells of the Stone People. They didn't know where the truth lay.

"Then you will bring us most precious stones," Heimir said, "your best stonemasons. You must start building a temple for Valtyr, so that we might bring His truth to this godless city."

Sugaoshi made zirself not react to that. The city of Killapany had a god. Kiproary. Sure, they didn't have many temples. All one had to do was to walk outside and see the holy mountain to be reminded of the bounty of their god.

Would these Bone People demand that they pull down the holy mountain next?

"It will be done," Mahletik said gravely.

Kinrahsy added, "I will put my best people on it."

When Heimir turned to Sugaoshi, ze said, "My artists will make it beautiful."

The other two councilmembers followed zir lead, promising their support.

The Bone People left the chamber happy. They had no idea that at least half the council wasn't under their control.

SUGAOSHI, Juhala, and Yagakilly all met in Juhala's office, officially to talk about their new project. The space felt cramped, with too many books on the shelves, too many papers on the desk, too little space for people to gather. At least any visitors to the office had a nice view of a beautiful garden outside, out the window behind Juhala's desk. Sugaoshi could see a couple of interesting stone statues, as well as a curving walkway.

They didn't meet outside, despite how much Sugaoshi's heart wanted to be in the bright sunlight after such darkness. Instead, they had gone indoors, someplace with a door that shut and locked, where they wouldn't be observed.

"Do you believe the nerve of those Bone People?" Yagakilly said, exploding with anger once they believed themselves to be safe. "How arrogant! To think that their god is the only one who matters."

None of the Stone People were that religious. Certainly not like the Sea People, who rang bells regularly during the day, calling everyone to stop whatever they were doing and pray. The Stone People did have a few temples, as well as regular services for those who needed them. There was also a large celebration for Kiproary in the spring, during the equinox. That was when the god would be most honored.

Not necessarily most remembered, however. Again, all

the Stone People had to do was step outside and look toward the holy mountain. That was all the prayer anyone needed.

"I think they are a young People," Sugaoshi said slowly. "They haven't been in contact with the other Peoples. They still have rough, abrasive edges, not smoothed off with contact from others."

Juhala nodded. "I agree," ze said. "They are like children."

"No, like teenagers," Yagakilly said. "They believe the world revolves around them. They have yet to grow up and learn that it doesn't."

Sugaoshi grimaced. That sounded exactly like all young people to zir. Then again, ze had never bothered with offspring. Ze had zir artwork instead. It didn't talk back.

"What are we going to do about Mahletik and Kinrahsy?" Yagakilly asked. "They've been infected. How are we going to defend the rest of our people?"

Sugaoshi had thought about this. "How did the pair of you defend yourselves?" ze asked. Ze looked at Juhala first.

Juhala shrugged. "I felt that darkness coming toward me and I deflected it."

"How?" Sugaoshi asked, surprised.

Juhala sighed. "It was like…like the first time I got close to a Wind Person who was rapidly flitting from one animal form to the next, showing off. A great whirlwind surrounded them. I knew that if I stepped too close, it would fill me, too. Uproot me. I'd never have another moment of peace if I let it get too close. So I deflected it." Ze sighed and shook zir head. "I don't know how to describe it. It was just a natural defense."

Sugaoshi tilted zir head to one side and considered the representative of the teachers. Did that mean that all of the teachers would be immune to the Bone People? Could they all naturally deflect that darkness, as they'd been in such close contact with the other people?

It was an avenue they'd have to explore later.

"And you?" Sugaoshi asked, turning towards Yagakilly.

"I burned it off," Yagakilly said. "Same as you."

Sugaoshi nodded. "Yes. You can use a spike of heat to stave off the infection." And that was what it was. An infection.

"Do you think if we could get Mahletik and Kinrahsy to spike their temperatures, that they could burn off their infection?" Juhala asked eagerly.

"It's too deep," Yagakilly said. "They may never get that darkness out of them."

Sugaoshi wasn't certain if that was the truth or not. "But surely they won't always be as suggestable," ze said. "It has to be a temporary effect. Or else they'll need regular infection."

"And who's to say that they won't be regularly infected? Particularly once they get this temple of theirs built?" Yagakilly asked.

Sugaoshi pictured in zir mind's eye—a dark tower, constantly spewing filth and dark clouds. Ze couldn't help but shiver.

"So how do we protect everyone else?" Juhala asked.

"We can warn our own constituents," Yagakilly said. "But only the ones from our districts. The ones from Mahletik and Kinrahsy cannot be warned. They have to risk being infected, as their representatives have been."

Sugaoshi sighed. Ze didn't like risking more people to the filth and control of the Bone People.

"Why don't we just find someone to kill the Bone People?" Juhala asked. "There's no reason to allow them to stay here any longer. We know that they aren't any good."

"Who could we find?" Sugaoshi asked. "None of the Stone People I know has ever killed someone before." It was very difficult to hurt a Stone Person. Certainly, accidents did occur and a Stone Person went to Ishkra before their time.

However, the punishment for murder was banishment—a truly horrific thought for most Stone People, so it worked well as a deterrent.

"We are stronger than they are," Yagakilly said slowly. "We could force them to leave."

"And what about the next group? And the next?" Sugaoshi pointed out. "No. We keep them here. Close to us. Observe them. Find their weaknesses so that we can exploit them. See how we can turn them all away, not just this group."

They had to take the long view here. Not just what was best for them during the next week, but over the next decade.

The other two councilmembers slowly nodded, agreeing with zir.

Sugaoshi shook zir head at zirself. Ze really had been spending too much time with the archives.

"When we warn our constituents, we need to tell them to start writing down everything they learn about the Bone People, no matter how insignificant," Juhala said. "Then compile the notes." Ze gave Sugaoshi a significant look at that. "Maybe the archivists can help."

"Don't you think the teachers would be best at that? Not the archivists?" Sugaoshi shot back. Ze didn't want to take on much more work or ze would never have time to paint again.

"The two groups should work together," Yagakilly suggested.

That sounded like a good compromise.

"I will also go and talk with a healer from the Sea People," Juhala said after a few moments. "See if they have any idea for how to deal with the infection in Mahletik and Kinrahsy."

"Good idea," Sugaoshi said, surprised that Juhala had thought of something as useful as that. Maybe Juhala wasn't as stupid as ze had always believed.

The Stone People didn't really have healers, not like the Wind or Sea People. They didn't get sick, didn't catch colds or have to deal with plagues sweep through their cities. They rarely broke limbs either. Generally, if a Stone Person stopped feeling well, they went to a specialist who would give them special minerals to rebalance their bodies.

Now that they had a plan, it was time to put it into action. Sugaoshi stood at the threshold of Juhala's office for a moment, hesitating.

Ze realized that ze was frightened to leave this sanctuary. Afraid of what ze might find outside.

Scared stiff that the Bone People might have already infected large swaths of the city.

No. Ze would not allow that.

Head held high, ze walked into the cold gray day, raising zir own internal temperature and ready to do battle for zir people.

Chapter Three

SEA

LISETH DREAMED of a Wind Person coming to see her. However, he was dressed strangely, in a blousy white top with a short yellow skirt. His brown hair was straight, and he had a box-like red hat perched on his head.

But his coloration was that of dried driftwood, and his face kept changing from person to animal—bear, rabbit, pig, hawk, and others.

He carried with him a tall golden goblet. The base flared out, and the sides were encrusted with beautiful emeralds and rubies. He gestured with it, like a scepter that someone in the royal family from an ancient age might have done.

Liseth couldn't understand what he was saying to her. The words kept getting garbled, particularly as he changed shapes. She understood the urgency underneath his tone, though.

He had an important message. Something she must know.

Finally, in desperation, the man went outside the temple, to the main fountain where Liseth liked to wash her feet. He stuck the cup under the water filling it.

When he lifted the cup back up, a small carp popped over the side, looking directly at her.

The carp spoke, using clear words that she could understand. It brought her greetings from Ajooless and asked how Liseth was doing.

Liseth replied that she was fine, and then asked after Ajooless' health and how the rest of the party was fairing.

One of the members of the group had died recently.

Liseth spoke her condolences, wondering if they were finally finished with the preliminaries.

Finally, just as the carp said, "I have an important message for you," Liseth felt herself waking. The dawn had come and sunlight was streaming across her bed.

Liseth fought to stay in the dream. Just being conscious of it woke her up further. The fish and the strange wind person disappeared.

Liseth stubbornly lay there with her eyes shut for a few moments, willing the dream to return. Eventually, she opened her eyes. The sun was not actually coming through her window. The day itself was cloudy and gray, with a fine misty rain. Liseth shivered as she looked around her bedroom. Like her office, it was practical, not showy. The narrow bed took up one entire wall, underneath the big window. A beautifully carved armoire took up most of the wall at the foot of the bed, full of dresses, official robes, and the rest of her clothes. Shelves stuffed with books, papers, and a few knickknacks lined the wall across from her. In the corner sat a comfortable reading chair.

Liseth's bedroom had always been her sanctuary. She never invited anyone else in here. Even the few times when she'd taken lovers, they'd always met somewhere else, not in her rooms.

Yet, even the thick glass windowpanes and the heavy

quilts on her bed couldn't keep the cold from seeping in that morning.

The dream had frightened her. Though Liseth didn't believe in foretellings, this dream had been too real.

Ajooless was trying to reach her, to contact her, to give her some news. As Gaynelus, the heroine of old, had done, Ajooless was trying to speak through the fish nearby to communicate…something.

But what?

DESPITE THE WORK piling up on Liseth's desk, she still left her office just after the midmorning prayer bells and went to the fish market closest to the temple. She didn't know if any of the merchants would carry carp, or if that was even the type of fish she needed.

The smell of fresh fish made Liseth's mouth water. While the Sea People ate seaweed and greens grown on shore, they also ate a lot of fish, served in many different ways. The underwater city specialized in brined and pickled fish as well as many types of raw fish. On land, the fish was often smoked or poached with herbs.

Liseth had had a lovely breakfast of seaweed stew, seasoned with tiny dried shrimp. Though that hadn't been too long ago, she was still hungry. She hadn't been eating regularly, too busy to leave her desk when the noon meal bells rang. Plus, her new assistant didn't have the confidence of Ajooless, who had sometimes come in to bully her boss into eating or taking a break.

Liseth slowly walked by the fish vendors, savoring the different meals they offered. The smell of a tangy tomato sauce made her mouth water, though so did the scent of smoked salmon.

Surely a midmorning snack wouldn't hurt her, right?

Liseth reminded herself that she wasn't here to please her stomach, but instead, was on a wild trout chase to find a magical fish.

She turned away from the aisle that served meals, walking to the parts of the market that sold live fish. The cheaper fish were all in barrels. Of course, they were well taken care of. No one would buy spoiled or sick creatures. The merchants used magic to support their fish, ensuring that the water was clean. The more expensive fish swam in long glass tanks, frequently lit with small magical globes to show off their beautiful scales.

More than one merchant sold carp, generally in barrels as they were one of the cheapest fish and were often from farms, not caught in the wild. They also had to be contained, as they'd grow huge if allowed to swim free.

Liseth walked up to each barrel, touching the side of it, seeing if one of the carp would come to the surface and talk with her. She felt foolish doing it, but that wasn't about to deter her from her task. She knew if she was successful, the fish merchant would be rich not just for her life, but for many generations.

However, none of the fish deigned to speak to her. Was Ajooless not trying to reach her now? Had she only tried this morning, while Liseth was still asleep? That didn't make any sense. Ajooless knew Liseth's schedule. She'd wait until Liseth was awake.

Disappointed, Liseth turned away from the common fish dealers to the merchants who dealt with the more exotic species. Some of the tanks held freshwater fish, but many contained ocean fish. They had to use a lot more magic to keep those tanks clean and the fish healthy, which just added to the cost.

Liseth didn't see the point in purchasing a fancy fish,

particularly one to eat. Maybe if she had a feast she were hosting…Then again, she didn't want to spend the temple funds unwisely. Unlike Bayaseth, the priestess of the main temple in the sea capital. Bayaseth would serve extremely expensive, exotic fish whenever she got a chance, as a way to remind others of the wealth and importance of the temple.

While Liseth believed the temple should be important because of the goddess they served, not because of the food they served.

But Liseth had lost that argument long ago, and didn't feel as though she should rehash it, even now.

The fish in the tanks were beautiful, at a time when Liseth felt she needed more beauty in her life. The bright blues of the blue tang with their brilliant yellow tails filled her with joy, as did the magnificently striped orange and white clown fish. She also really liked the reds, pinks and golds of the scalefin, as well as the more muted colors of the parrotfish.

None of these fish were for food, but for people who had their own tanks in their homes.

Liseth was just about to leave the market, maybe head back to one of the vendors and perhaps have a small snack, some of the prawns in the lemon-garlic sauce, when a large tank caught her eye.

It was filled with goldfish of many different colors. Liseth found her feet walking toward it. She was fascinated by the black one that had a neon blue mouth, as well as the ones spotted black and white, like some sort of cow. The salmon and gold ones were pretty, but the prettiest one practically shimmered in the tank, its white, gold, and red scales in an interesting pattern.

"Can I help you, my lady?" asked the fish merchant diffidently.

Liseth glanced over at the person. She was shorter than

most of the Sea People by a good head. She also had a girth that not many of the Sea People ever gained. She looked more like a Wind Person in many respects, as her skin had gone gray with age. The bony crest over the top of her head was prominent, and her eyes were set too far apart, giving her a squid-like appearance. She wore a plain brown dress with a solid black apron over it, as most of the merchants did.

"I'm not sure," Liseth said slowly. She found her eyes kept going back to the spotted goldfish, the one with the interesting patterns on its sides. If she were feeling fanciful—well, even more fanciful than searching for a talking carp—she'd say the colors and patterns kept changing.

"What can you tell me about that one?" she asked, pointing to what was turning out to be her favorite fish.

"Ah, him," the merchant said. "He's a wily one, that one. I raise me fish in a pond. I don't always keep good count of 'em, as many die off in the winter. Never count yer fish before spring, that's what I say." She gave a wide grin to Liseth, who merely noted that the Sea Person was missing a few teeth.

"Anyway, the fish change colors sometimes as they age. Some get brighter, some duller. This one, I thought I'd lost 'im. And he was so pretty, too! But I couldn't find him as I was getting ready for market. At least for two years. Then, this spring, up he pops, coming out of nowhere! Not sure where he's been hiding." The merchant turned to talk directly to the fish. "Ye were just biding your time, I know. Waiting to show off for the perfect lady."

That made Liseth smile. Was there any truth to the tale? Probably not. Though the fish merchant didn't strike Liseth as all that intelligent.

"So how much for the fancy boy?" Liseth asked, preparing herself for a strong bargain.

The merchant looked Liseth up and down shrewdly.

"Normally, I'd be charging a pretty penny for such a pretty boy, large and handsome as he is," she said. "But I think ye were meant to be together. He'll be the pride of any pond, and happy to show off for ye."

Liseth blinked, astonished. Surely it wasn't about to be that easy.

Then the merchant quoted a price that literally took Liseth's breath away.

Only after a long, heated session did Liseth get the price down to about half of what the merchant originally quoted. It was still far, far too much for such a common fish.

The merchant bagged up the fish easily. It swam right into her net, as if it knew that it was going home with Liseth.

Liseth had to stop and rest many times as she carried the small bucket filled with water and almost overflowing with the fish on her way back to the temple. Every time she stopped, she asked herself: what the hell was she doing? She had no use for a fish. She had no personal tank.

There was a goldfish pond in the back of the temple. She didn't visit it often. Would they mind another fish there?

Liseth still felt foolish at having spent so much money on a common goldfish.

The only thought that made her feel better was that goldfish were a type of carp, which had been the fish in her dream.

Now, she just had to visit the carp when Ajooless was trying to contact her. Maybe she'd finally get the important message that her dream had hinted at.

THE GOLDFISH POND was larger than Liseth remembered, at least twenty feet around. Most of the fish were dormant, as it was still winter. A very large fountain splashed to one side of the pond, keeping the waters fresh and clean. Benches lined it as well, for people to come and sit and possibly commune with the fish.

Liseth had never really spent time staring into the pond, though she noticed many of her acolytes came to visit often, as she herself came back again and again throughout the next two days.

It was sometime after the midafternoon bells on the third day that Liseth felt her head drooping, her eyes closing as she sat in the wan sunshine. She hadn't felt tired just a few moments before, and now she couldn't keep herself awake.

Instead of fighting it, Liseth stayed seated where she was. She could indulge herself in a short break before going back to her office.

As soon as she closed her eyes, she saw the special carp swim over to the edge of the water and stick its head out to address her.

"You're here!" came the breathless words.

"Ajooless," Liseth said, nodding. "What important message do you have for me?" she asked immediately, foregoing all the polite necessities.

"The Bone People are on their way to the city," the acolyte said. "They should be arriving in a day or so. You should meet them warmly. Organize trade with them."

Liseth blinked, surprised. How were the Bone People traveling so quickly? Why hadn't they been spotted? Then again, there weren't many overland roads that went up and down the coast. The Sea People primarily swam when they went north or south, though occasionally they used boats as well.

"I will greet them with honor," Liseth said formally. Though the Wind People bragged about their hospitality, Liseth knew that the Sea People easily matched it.

"They are curious about our great city," Ajooless said.

"You need to show them all the sights, the beautiful fountains and markets. Be sure to bring them to the temple of your sister as well."

Liseth blinked, surprised. What did Ajooless mean? The Bone People couldn't breathe under the water, could they?

"My group will continue east, to the lands of the Wind People," Ajooless said after another moment. "Goodbye." Then the contact was broken.

Liseth sat up and opened her eyes, surprised.

Swimming just under the water was the brightly colored fish that she'd bought from the market. He disappeared quickly, going back to the bottom of the pond for the rest of his long winter nap.

The fish hadn't actually lifted his head above the water to speak to her. That would have killed him, being out of the water for so long. Yet, Ajooless had still used the fish, somehow, to speak to her from so far away, as Gaynelus had in the legends.

Despite her excitement, Liseth also felt chilled and wary.

There was something else going, something that Ajooless couldn't say about the Bone People. She'd been trying to not only get a message to Liseth, but a warning as well, hence the nonsense about bringing the Bone People to her sister's temple.

Liseth went over the message, remembering every word. It sounded to her as though the Ajooless and the others had already met the Bone People.

Had they been standing there while Ajooless communicated with Liseth? Forcing her to say things? Was that why Ajooless had told Liseth that the Bone People came as friends? When in fact, they were probably enemies?

Something was going on here. Something bad.

Liseth was just going to have to prepare for the worst. Including the possibility that the third age was about to end and all the Peoples would die, and the gods would help.

LISETH DIDN'T WANT to panic her people. However, she needed to get as many of them as she could out of the land city of Shiboleth and into the water, to the twin sea city of Sillboden.

She didn't know for a fact that the Bone People couldn't live under the water. However, she would bet that was the case, that that had been the warning that Ajooless had been trying to give her.

How much time did she have? She couldn't arrange an orderly retreat of everyone in the city and she didn't want to panic her people, particularly if there was no cause. Instead, she had to prioritize who would leave and who would be left behind, so she took it in stages.

After sending messengers to Bayaseth, warning her of the waves of people who would need shelter, as well as warning the Stone People of the Sea People's predicament, Liseth organized her acolytes and sent them to all the schools. Their instructions were to tell the teachers that a national water holiday had just been declared and all the children needed to spend the day in the sea.

When the parents came later that day to pick up the children, they could also be escorted to the waters.

Next, Liseth sent hunters overland, to the south, looking for the Bone People. Maybe they could be stopped for a day or so before they reached the city. She organized a second group of hunters to stay with her in the temple. She'd never felt the need for guards before. They would escort her when she went to meet the Bone People.

After warning the council of regents about the Bone

People, as well as her fears, Liseth started informing the various merchant guilds that it was time to leave the city, beginning with the fish merchants and the farmers who grew seaweed.

Liseth almost felt as though she was underwater with the currents of people flowing in and out of her office.

Just after the midafternoon prayer bells rang, one of the scouts that Liseth had sent to the south returned.

"They're less than an hour away," Katamesh said sternly. Like most males, his skin was a blue-gray, instead of the whitish blue of the females. However, the shock of his message had paled his skin further. He wore a sleeveless green tunic that reached his thighs, along with long gray pants that reached his ankles. Unlike most of the Sea People, he wore actual boots, not sandals. Then again, he frequently went overland and needed to protect his feet.

"Can we at least greet them outside the city?" Liseth asked, rising.

"Yes, if you hurry," Katamesh said. He stood stiffly in front of her desk, his long javelin still in his hand.

Liseth grimaced and started reeling off orders to the acolytes who still attended her. They'd gotten the children out of the city and many of the guild members had left as well. However, they would now have to stop the flight of people leaving the city. She didn't want to appear to be in a panic.

However, she still arranged for people to continue to flow toward the sea in a steady trickle.

She sent a quick prayer to Ishkra then went with the scout, out to meet her destiny.

THE APPEARANCE of the Bone People surprised her. She

knew that they'd be all white from Ka Lem's description of them. However, the skin of the face of some of the ones who approached the city had a more golden appearance. In addition, their hair was yellow-gold, though some were darker and others were more red.

Gold was always the color of wisdom for the Sea People, the color the soul took on, losing the white of innocence as it was reborn again and again, washed in Ishkra's waters.

Did these people have more wisdom than she and her sisters?

Liseth knew that without Ajooless' warning, she would have greeted them with great respect and allowed them access to the innermost sacred sanctuaries of the city.

As it was, she stood out on a grassy plain that was just south of the city. There were no walls around the city—Shiboleth had never been attacked and had never needed such. There was a large gate arching over the trade road, carved out of the same white stone as the arches on the piers leading to the sea. Sea turtles, otters, eels, sharks, and whales were done in bas relief on the edges and the top. During the celebrations of the goddess's birthday, it would be draped with seaweed and fragrant woven reeds.

While some of the two dozen Bone People walked, many rode on the long, four-wheeled carts being drawn by dead elk. The bone creatures were frightening to behold. The impression that Liseth had was that the bones of the animals weren't pure, despite how bleached white they appeared. Instead, there was a corruption there, deep in the marrow. The bucks all walked awkwardly, their heads dipping constantly with their backwards antlers.

It was the eyes of the elk that made Liseth want to retch. They burned with an unquenchable fire that would light up the world, igniting anything flammable.

Fortunately, it was the middle of winter, and the grasses

were all wet. Still, the trail smoldered where the elk had passed.

It made Liseth shiver, recalling the myths about the ending of the third age, her age, with fire.

Liseth stood with half a dozen hunters arrayed behind her, half female, half male. All wore long pants and boots instead of the sandals that most of the Sea People wore. It was odd how the Bone People were fully clothed, from their necks to wrists and ankles. Their clothing didn't look very comfortable. And it would have been completely impractical in the water.

Which told Liseth the truth: that Ajooless had been trying to send a warning with the comment about taking the Bone People to visit her sister's temple.

Liseth slowly moved one of her hands behind her and clenched her fist, letting the hunters know to be extra wary of these people.

If only she'd had more time to move the majority of her people out into the sea! From there, they would have been able to come up with an appropriate plague to wipe out not just the Bone People who'd invaded her city, but all of them, tracing the waters back to their homeland.

For now, Liseth played the part of the gracious host. She must stop short of all-out war between the Bone People and the Sea People, else they tempt the gods to step in and kill them all.

After the carts came to a halt, all the Bone People came slowly forward in a group. The one who faced Liseth was probably a male, given his had broad shoulders that went down to a narrow waist.

He didn't seem nervous facing Liseth. Maybe wary was a better description.

Liseth kept her smile warm. Was it just because the Sea People looked so much different than all the others? They had no hair, but instead, a bony ridge that ran from the middle of their skull down to their neck. Their eyes tended to be set wider apart, and their skin was bluish-white. They were the tallest of all the Peoples, frequently well over six feet, thin and willowy. The Stone People were the strongest of all the Peoples, with the Wind People next and the Sea People the weakest. However, they grew more muscles when they went into the water and transformed.

"I am Liseth, the high priestess of the goddess Ishkra," Liseth said.

"I am Gunnar," he said. He wore an off-white shirt, black trousers, and thick black boots. Around his waist hung a beautiful brown leather belt. The curling designs embossed around the edges of it reminded Liseth of waves. "I am the high priest of the god Valtyr."

Liseth stifled her first impulse, which was to giggle madly.

A fourth god? Oh yes. The end times were near at hand if she didn't move very, very carefully.

<hr>

THE BLACKNESS that swirled up from the Bone People didn't completely surprise Liseth. She'd been anticipating some sort of attack, something that would sap her will. The squid-ink like cloud covered her in filth and drained the bright green from the world.

However, Liseth felt herself split in two as the abyss wrapped itself around her. While a part of her nodded and agreed to everything the Bone People said—that she would build them a large temple for their god, replacing the one dedicated to Ishkra—a part of her was separate, watching everything and waiting for a chance…to do what, Liseth wasn't certain.

The hunters arrayed behind Liseth all appeared to have the same spell cast on them. Were they split too? None appeared to be able to withstand the suggestions placed on them by the Bone People.

With heavy feet, Liseth turned and led the way back to the city. She wanted to rail against how unfair it was! Didn't Gunnar and the others realize what a dangerous game they were playing? They'd fail in their bid to conquer all the lands and the gods would come down and sweep the world clean with fire.

Probably using the unnatural elk and their eternal flame to do it.

A large fountain splashed merrily just past the beautiful archway. Without thinking about it, Liseth walked directly over to the water and stuck her feet in. It was partly to wash away the filthy squid-ink cloud that she felt clinging to her skin as much as sheer habit.

As soon as the water touched her skin, Liseth woke all the way up. She kept her face slack, but she finally understood Ajooless' warning.

The Bone People didn't understand that their spell only worked on the land form of the Sea People. It was why Liseth had felt as though she'd split her consciousness in two. The sea form swam free of the Bone People's magic.

All Liseth had to do was to stick some part of herself—hands, feet, head—into the water, and be washed clean.

For a moment, Liseth considered ordering the hunters to round up the Bone People. They'd have to find a deep dark cellar to put them in, as well as keep a running river across the entrance so that a Sea Person would have to step in the water before being able to unlock the door.

However, the hunters all wore boots, not sandals. None of them could wash themselves clean. They were still completely enslaved by the Bone People.

If she didn't do exactly as Gunnar said, he might order her own hunters to attack her.

And they might do it.

Liseth pretended to still be under the control of the Bone People as she led them through the city. Many of her own people lined the main road, clicking and hissing in surprise. Gunnar and the others walked with such arrogance! Liseth felt ashamed for them.

As part of her preparation, Liseth had emptied the school where the Wind and Stone People stayed when visiting the Sea People. There was a yard for the elk to stay in, though they didn't need the watering troughs or hay set aside for the oxen favored by the Stone People when they traveled.

She left the Bone People there, her own corrupted hunters guarding them.

Who knew how many the Bone People would turn against her before she managed to stop them?

And how was she going to do that, when they could sap the will of any of the Sea People? Their control wouldn't last, but they might be able to do a tremendous amount of damage in a short amount of time. And what other powers did they have? What other tricks might they pull to keep the Sea People compliant?

Liseth didn't want to run away. Didn't want to lose her home. But until she figured out how to stop the Bone People without all-out war, the Sea People might abandon her beloved city.

Chapter Four

WIND

KA LEM FOUGHT the corruption of the Bone People, the inky darkness that filled his soul with filth that came pouring out from Diethelm, the priest of Valtyr who stayed with them. He visited the prisoners every morning and every evening, preaching to them about the power of his god and how they, the Wind People, needed to learn their place, as well as the inferiority of their god, Sune Li.

Every time the weight of the abyss landed on Ka Lem, it pushed down on him so hard it was difficult for him to stay standing. His will was being sapped as well. Eventually, he'd be unable to resist. He would do anything the Bone People asked him to do.

He would forget how to dance.

Most of the other prisoners, a half dozen Wind People, had already succumbed. As far as Ka Lem could tell, only he and Ma Qi, one of the travel elders, still resisted. They talked occasionally, using the wind language of the elders, their words landing in each other's ears with no one else able to hear.

The king of the Bone People—King Einar—no longer

traveled with their group, but had gone further south with most of the original party, leaving the Wind People to the tender care of Diethelm. At least they'd finally been given some clothing—not because the Wind People had ever felt shame regarding their naked bodies, but because it was winter and cold.

Except…part of Diethelm's "training" was that they should be ashamed of their nakedness, that they needed to be covered up all the time, that showing so much skin was somehow inherently wrong.

Ka Lem and the prisoners stayed where they were, while waves of Bone People arrived and left, continuing to the west. The force making its way to the lands of the Wind People filled Ka Lem with even more than his usual dread. Hundreds of warriors were approaching, armed with knives and nets.

Why had the Bone People maintained this one base? Keeping the prisoners here? The mood around camp was one of waiting.

But for what?

Most of the guards in the camp slept all day long, then patrolled constantly at night. The few that stayed awake dug pits all around the group, then covered them over with tarps and grass, hiding them.

It finally occurred to Ka Lem that the Bone People were setting a trap.

His heart stirred. Were some of his fellow travelers coming and freeing the prisoners? Of course they were. He hadn't considered the possibility because his thoughts had grown so slow from Diethelm's ministrations. Plus, he wasn't getting enough food or water. His stomach felt like a leaden weight, hanging off the rest of his body, always empty. He was going to be down to just skin and bones soon, a walking skeleton, like the elk.

He talked with Ma Qi about how to warn any potential rescuers of the danger, not just from the Bone People, but from their own as well.

Would the other prisoners start yelling if someone came to free them in the night?

Ma Qi sighed, the wind carrying the sound but not the emotion. Ka Lem assumed she felt as sad as he did. He couldn't be angry with his fellow prisoners. He didn't blame them either. He only wished they'd also found a way to resist.

Not all the Wind People can hear the wind language, Ma Qi reminded Ka Lem. *And I can only speak to those nearby.*

Ka Lem stayed perfectly still, though he wanted to nod, to show acknowledgement of the message received. He didn't know how far his own range went, though he suspected that he was stronger than the older person. However, he only knew the basics of the wind language, whatever lessons Ma Qi could secretly teach him. Since his other prisoners had turned, they would sometimes report to the Bone People when a conversation was happening on the wind, words that their captors couldn't hear.

We will both try if we hear a disturbance in the night, Ka Lem said eventually.

There wasn't much else they could do. Except sit and wait with the rest of the camp, brooding over the dark future that lay ahead of them.

NIGHT. Ka Lem had always focused on the stars before, the light of the two moons. He'd never paid that much attention to the quality of the night, the feel of the darkness.

Since being captured by the Bone People and exposed to their filth, Ka Lem felt much more aware of the darkness than ever before. He couldn't see better in the dark, which surprised him. He'd been afraid that the Bone People who worshiped the abyss would have great night vision. As far as Ka Lem could tell, they couldn't see any better than his people in the dark.

The Stone People could still see the best at night, and if they were leading the rescue teams, they might have a chance of avoiding the pits.

Ka Lem felt the night caress his skin, pressing up against it like a cold lover trying to get warm. It would never let him go, and he could never truly get warm himself. There was no escaping it.

In order to brighten his spirits, Ka Lem would shuffle his feet the tiniest bit. Most of the motion was actually in his head, just remembering what it felt like to dance.

Almost every night—and they'd been there for five days now—it grew progressively harder to remember the dance, to feel the lightness that had once filled his spirit. He'd never been a particularly graceful dancer, but the bear deep inside him refused to give up.

The magical chain linking the prisoners' feet together prevented them from changing into any animal forms. All of them had scabbed skin where their metal shackles rubbed, frequently raw and bleeding.

If rescuers could break the chain, would Ka Lem even remember how to change form? How long would it take him?

He held the form of a great black-headed goose at the ready, forcing himself to recall how it felt for his body to collapse in on itself as the change began, how his neck elongated and his fingers fused while feathers pushed their way out of his skin. Weight would shift from his legs up into his torso, so his ankles would grow thin and he could step out of the damned shackles that held him. The world would change, colors muting while other senses took over.

As a goose, he didn't have an acute sense of smell. However, he would suddenly scent any open water very well, and would be able to accurately predict how far away it was. In addition, a sense that he didn't have as a Wind Person would develop, and even with his eyes closed he would know which direction was north.

Despite knowing that a goose was the best choice of animal when the rescue came, a part of him wanted instead to transform into the bear who kept his soul warm. However, while she'd be able to rend and tear at the guards, she wouldn't be able to take off and flee as quickly as a bird. Plus, she'd be more vulnerable to the nets thrown by the Stone People.

The evening of the fifth day of their imprisonment brought little relief from the cold and hunger. Ka Lem huddled with the other prisoners, shivering. The guards made fun of them piled together like animals, but really, what did they expect when the nights grew so cold and they had no warm clothes or blankets?

At least it helped keep Ka Lem awake, his senses stretched out far across the camp, seeking…something.

It was nights like these that Ka Lem found himself reaching for the wind. Gan Ou had said that there was a place inside of herself where magic could go, a pocket that just needed to be filled. Over the past few days of idleness, Ka Lem had time to find similar places inside of himself, holes that at one point would have been filled with magic if he'd lived in a different age and time.

Though his people had been called the Wind People from the earliest age, Ka Lem wondered why they'd been given that name. They changed into animal forms. Why weren't they called the Animal People?

Surely they could do something with the wind. Something magical to protect themselves. He caught fleeting glimpses of it sometimes as he hoovered on the edge of sleep, a swirling column of leaves that could be used to do…something.

Ka Lem found that night growing more still than the others. It was five days from midwinter, and the official celebrations of Sune Li and the coming of the light.

Would there be any feasts for him? When did the Bone People celebrate their god? Was it during the summer solstice, when the darkness began to creep back into the world?

A noise in the distance brought Ka Lem fully awake. It was a sound that had no place in the quiet night. The sound of a quiet footstep nearby.

He used the wind language to tell Ma Qi.

They're here.

Then he pushed out a whirling wind of warning. It surprised him that it was strong enough to form an actual breeze, swirling around all the prisoners.

Could he call up a stronger wind someday? When he wasn't shackled and his power drained?

The chain that connected the prisoners together didn't allow them much movement. It kept them in a specific order as well. Ka Lem was at one end, and Nu Zhay was on the other.

Movement to the left of Ka Lem drew his attention slowly. He didn't abruptly turn his head, didn't want to alert any of the guards or his fellow prisoners.

Someone knelt next to the huge weight that the chain of the Wind People was linked to. Ka Lem couldn't say why but he felt certain that it was a Stone Person. There wasn't enough light for him to see who it was.

He pushed out again, trying to send his winds toward zir, wanting to warn whoever it was of the danger.

The Stone Person stirred as the winds swirled around them, looking in his direction and nodding.

Ka Lem watched, fascinated as the Stone Person placed zir palm against the iron chain, pushing down on it. He knew that the Stone People could heat things with zir hands. Would zir be able to heat the metal to the breaking point?

No. He thought he caught a glimpse of blue when the Stone Person released the chain, then smashed down on it with all zir strength.

The frozen links shattered with a loud tinkling noise. A second soft crash followed from the other side of the chain.

Suddenly, guards appeared, their nets at the ready.

"Run! Beware the pits!" Ka Lem called out before he started to transform.

It filled his heart with gladness that the other Wind People, despite their corruption, were still trying to escape. He felt more than saw the swirling winds of transformation as the others changed.

Ka Lem concentrated again on the form of the goose. It was hard for him to find, as he'd suspected it would be. He still pushed toward it, expecting to feel the weight of the nets landing on him at any time.

But the guards weren't focused on the prisoners. Instead, they piled onto the Stone People at either end of the line.

Ka Lem withdrew his feet from the shackles. He suddenly felt like *himself* again, as his bare feet touched the earth.

The Stone Person to his left was fighting off the guards, throwing them as they bodily tried to knock zir to the ground. But ze would be overwhelmed soon.

Ka Lem suddenly felt sick to his stomach.

The guards weren't trying to stop any of the prisoners. No, they'd served their purpose as bait for the two Stone People.

Ka Lem marveled at zir strength as the Stone Person picked up a guard and flung him to the side, then a second.

The Stone Person lying on the ground cut at the nets holding zir with a dark blade.

Ka Lem had almost reached his full goose form. He could escape in just a few short moments.

And leave those that rescued him to the Bone People.

With a loud quack, Ka Lem shook himself.

That wasn't right.

Quicker, much quicker than before, Ka Lem transformed himself into the familiar bear shape. He waded into the fight, happy to discover that his claws and teeth easily dug into the flesh of the guards. He'd been afraid that the darkness would somehow give them a magical protection, that he wouldn't be able to fight them.

But they were merely flesh and bone. And he was angry.

He'd never hurt a person before, not like this. He wanted to blame the filth that the Bone People had piled up on his soul for making it so easy. He knew better, though. This was part of him, too.

Did he kill any of those he knocked to the side? Probably. If not immediately, their wounds would fester if they didn't get proper medical treatments.

Ka Lem couldn't help the Stone Person who was still cutting zir way out of the nets piled up. He could only chase the guards away, while at the same time trying to avoid their nets himself.

The other Stone Person helped with that by pulling off the one net that did get thrown over Ka Lem.

Finally, the stone person on the ground was able to stand up.

The rest of the Wind People had left. Ka Lem was glad they'd been freed.

However, it would be a slow walk out of the camp, back to the thick wall of fog. The Stone People couldn't move fast.

Before he could transform into a much larger creature, who might have the strength to carry them both, more guards came running up. There were over a dozen, now. Ka Lem growled low and deep in his throat, a sound that he knew would raise the hackles of all those who faced him.

The guards paused, lifting their nets.

"Now!" came the command.

The guards all threw their nets simultaneously.

The Stone People held their arms up as the nets fell, their hands glowing red in the dark night. The nets burned as they fell, some falling to pieces. The nets that remained intact started smoldering when they came into contact with the Stone People's bodies.

Ka Lem tried to use his wind to keep the nets from him, but he found that he couldn't raise one in his animal form. It must be a power that only his person form could use.

Still, Ka Lem reared up onto his hindlegs and clawed at the nets, slashing and tearing the first one.

More fell, carrying Ka Lem to the ground.

The closest Stone Person reached down and flung the nets away from zir before ze passed out. "Flee!" ze said urgently.

Ka Lem shook his head as he pulled himself up. No. He would not abandon his rescuers.

He still shrank himself down into a mountain lion, the quickest and fiercest form he could think of. He raced away, between two of the guards, stretching his legs and gaining speed as he banked in a sharp curve and returned, pouncing and driving the first guard he came across to the ground, then running away again before they could catch him.

On his next pass, the guards were ready, some facing out while some still focused on the Stone People. Ka Lem avoided the nets on this pass, tearing at the legs of one of the guards before fleeing again.

If only Ka Lem was older, and had been able to study more! Then he could take the form of a flock of little birds. The nets would pass right over him and be unable to hold him. He wouldn't be able to do much to help the Stone People in that form, though.

He didn't consider running away, however. He returned to make a third pass.

As he neared, one of the Stone People suddenly disappeared.

Ze had fallen into one of the pits.

Ka Lem stopped beside the dark opening, growling, his tail lashing from side to side. But he couldn't protect the Stone Person until ze climbed out of the pit.

Maybe if he kept the guards away for long enough, the Stone Person could tunnel zir way out, though…

The second Stone Person faded into the night. Ka Lem didn't see them go. He wished them luck as the nets fell again, carrying Ka Lem into darkness.

***

THE GROUND WAS SHAKING as Ka Lem awoke. For a moment, he thought he was in a terrific storm and the thunder was so loud the ground quaked in response.

But the swaying motion felt wrong. The surface underneath him was hard. Was he in a hammock? He'd never been on a boat, though the Sea People had often described being on a boat as a feeling of rocking.

No. He was on a cart. The familiar weight of iron shackles around his ankles made his spirits sink deeper.

Where were the Bone People taking him?

He blinked his eyes open looking straight up at the clear

sky. It was midmorning. He'd been unconscious since the night before. The sun seemed brighter in the pale blue sky than it had since he'd drawn close to the wall. He sniffed. The smell of smoke had faded.

Ka Lem forced himself to sit up. Though he didn't know for certain, he'd say that they weren't heading west, but east. The air was fresher as they left the wall of smoke behind.

Where were they going? Why were they going east?

Ka Lem's feet were back in shackles, with a chain connecting them, which was then attached to huge iron loops bolted to the wood of the cart. Ka Lem faced backwards. Supplies piled high at the front of the cart blocked his view of the driver or where they were going. A rough blanket covered his nakedness. He was still starving, and felt gross and dirty.

Another cart traveled beside him across the broad open meadows. Like his, supplies were all piled up at the front of it, but a mound of rocks had been assembled at the back of it, under a heap of weighted nets.

With a start, Ka Lem suddenly realized it was a Stone Person, Daleki, the other teacher, a friend of Noalanon's. Ze didn't appear to be awake.

Ka Lem's heart felt lighter. While it would have been nice to have a friend to talk with, Noalanon didn't deserve the fate that awaited them.

Whatever that might be.

He didn't know for certain how many carts traveled together. There were a couple more behind him, but he couldn't see how many were before him, blocked from his view by the piles of boxes and trunks. Each cart was drawn by two dead elk, who left wisps of fire in their wake.

When the carts stopped moving a short while later, the driver came to the back and handed Ka Lem a hunk of bread, as well as a leather water pouch. It was more food than

Ka Lem had seen for days. He tore into the bread like an animal, ashamed of himself for not breaking off pieces and eating them with his fingers, but he was so hungry.

"I'm Anjr," the driver said, introducing herself. She swallowed the second half of her name, similar to how Valtyr was pronounced. She had long golden hair that she wore tied back in a tight braid, though little hairs had escaped and frizzed around her long face. Her eyes were pale gray, wide and open, giving her an innocent look. She wore a long-sleeved gray shirt over a set of brown wool trousers, with solid black boots. None of it looked that well-made or comfortable. Over that, she wore a plain leather vest lined with fur. Her cloth belt looked woven out of a sturdy material, white with stripes of pale green and red running the length of it.

It had taken Ka Lem a while to distinguish between the males and females of the Bone People. They all wore their hair the same—long and tied back—as well as the same clothing that covered them from head to toe. The males were the ones with the tooled leather belts. The fancier the designs, the more important they appeared to be, while the females tended to wear cloth belts and had many little bags hanging from it.

The females drove the carts and took care of the elk, and the males primarily worked as guards. The females were also the cooks and appeared to do many of the chores around the camp.

While the Wind and the Stone People all did the same work regardless of their gender, the Sea People had many tasks that were gender-specific: the males looked after the children and made most of the food while the females were the priestesses and the merchants.

When Ka Lem realized that the guard was staring at him,

he finally slowed down his desperate gnawing and said, "I'm Ka Lem."

The smile she gave him surprised him. Was she trying to be friendly? She would be the first of the Bone People who was.

"Where are we going?" he asked after another few hasty bites.

"Back to Melefels," she said proudly.

"Is that your capital?" Ka Lem said slowly, trying not to show his astonishment that someone was actually talking to him.

"'Tis," Anjr said. She gave him a grin, showing her broad, flat teeth. It was another way that the Bone People appeared different than the other Peoples. Their mouths seemed extra wide, as if they had many more teeth. But the teeth themselves weren't sharp or pointed, not like the Sea People's. They reminded Ka Lem more of oxen teeth than any other form.

"I've never been there," Anjr continued as Ka Lem took a long swig of water from the leather pouch. The taste was pure and sweet. Ka Lem had to stop himself from drinking all of it in a single gulp. "I grew up in Wesestanda, a small village north of the capital. Where did you grow up?"

"Ju Yen," Ka Lem said automatically.

"Where's that?" Anjr asked innocently.

Ka Lem narrowed his eyes at her. What was she playing at? He had the feeling that there was more to her questioning than he'd originally believed.

It wasn't the laws of hospitality that drove her, or he wouldn't be sitting here, a prisoner, and chained to their cart.

"West of the capital," Ka Lem lied easily. "About two days' run." He wasn't about to give his captors accurate information about the lands of the Wind People, information that they might be able to use against him.

Anjr was about to ask another question when shouted voices drew their attention.

A guard had gotten too close to Daleki, who'd grabbed hold of his arm with a super-heated hand. Ze was forced to let go when a guard used one of the Stone People's own black obsidian knives against zir, slicing open zir hardened skin.

"I've never seen such people before," Anjr said, leaning closer to Ka Lem and speaking very softly. "Stone People! King Einar had warned that there were strange creatures here in the lands of the pagans."

"Pagans?" Ka Lem asked, unfamiliar with the term.

Anjr turned to him, her gray eyes wide. "You're a pagan," she explained. "Because you don't believe in the one god."

"Even you know that more than one god exists," Ka Lem said, worried.

"But only one is important," Anjr insisted.

Ka Lem shook his head. "Every People have their own god," he said. "And each believe that their god is the most important. However, we're taught from an early age to respect others' beliefs."

Anjr said cheerily, "You're wrong. You'll learn better."

Ka Lem opened his mouth then shut it again. Ignorance was one thing. Refusing to learn or respect another was something else entirely.

He finally slowed down his eating enough that he could start breaking off pieces of bread and chewing at them slowly while he thought. Anjr obviously had other questions for him. He didn't look at her to encourage her, at least while he tried to wrap his head around an entire People who thought they were superior.

No, not that they thought they were superior. Who were willing to act on their superiority, willing to go to war in order to prove it to the rest of the People.

When Ka Lem finally raised his head and looked at Anjr, she asked, "Why won't she eat?"

"Who?" Ka Lem asked, looking around. Was there another prisoner here? Trapped on another cart?

"Her," Anjr said, pointing at the stone person.

Daleki sat up now on the cart, looking straight ahead and ignoring the driver standing there.

"Zir," Ka Lem corrected absentmindedly. "What are you trying to feed zir?"

"Zir?" Anjr said, puzzled.

"A Stone Person has no gender," Ka Lem said. "They are not "him" or "her" but zir."

Anjr looked shocked. "*It* won't eat the bread we give it."

Ka Lem didn't like the stubborn look around her jaw. Or how she'd decided to label Daleki as a thing.

"Ze doesn't eat bread," Ka Lem said. "Ze needs special minerals. Or ze will starve to death."

"They eat dirt?" Anjr said.

"No," Ka Lem said firmly. "Special minerals. They have to carry their own food with them when they travel to our lands." He paused, then added, "You're going to have to let zir go. Or ze will starve to death."

Anjr continued to look stubborn as she walked away to talk with Daleki's cart driver.

Ka Lem didn't have high hopes for the Stone Person's survival. He tried to use the wind language, to speak to zir, but ze didn't appear to hear him.

After a few moments, Ka Lem reached for the winds deep inside of him. He pushed out a breeze, stirring the Stone Person's hair slightly.

Daleki turned zir head, staring at him.

He pushed a slight breeze toward zir again.

Daleki smiled at him. It was a sad smile. Ka Lem felt his own heart ache in response.

It was the smile of an elder, at peace with zirself, committed to die.

KA LEM'S gut wrenched as guards looped ropes around Daleki's arms and torso, holding zir back. It took half a dozen strong men on each limb to hold zir still.

He'd felt helpless before, but nothing like this. He wanted to howl and bar his teeth, but he couldn't transform, couldn't save zir, could only watch.

Finally, another Bone Person who Ka Lem hadn't seen before walked forward carrying a long iron bar, about two inches square and three feet long. She had an extremely fancy and expensive cloth belt, dyed black with gold embroidery around the edges. Her hair was still mostly blonde, but gray was starting to encroach on it. Her clothing seemed better made as well, the shirt a soft white linen, the trousers a sturdy black wool, and solid black boots. She also wore a leather apron to protect herself.

After Daleki was immobilized, this female attached the iron bar to the shackles around Daleki's ankles. She didn't use any tools that Ka Lem could see. Instead, she molded the iron, weaving the links together with her bare hands.

Ka Lem had watched both glass workers from the Sea People as well as rock workers from the Stone People do the same; take raw material and shape it with magic. It appeared that working iron was the Bone People's primary ability. Some of the Wind People could do the same with wood, though very few had that touch.

He looked down at the shackles that covered his own ankles. No wonder he'd never been able to find a hinge! The iron had been melded into place, probably by this Bone Person.

The iron worker attached first one, then the other of Daleki's wrists to the iron bar. The Stone Person would be able to feed zirself, but ze wouldn't be able to grab hold of another guard and burn them as ze had: ze no longer had the range of motion.

"Who's that?" Ka Lem asked Anjr as the iron worker finished.

"Sutja," Anjr said with a grimace. "She thinks she's too high and mighty to cook with the others. Considers it beneath her."

It appeared that the iron worker wasn't held in high regard, despite her abilities.

"Why do the females cook?" Ka Lem said, curious. Was it because they had some special skill or ability?

Anjr looked blankly at him. "Because that's how it's always been done," she said simply.

Ka Lem shrugged. "The best cook in the family prepares the meals among my people. Same with the Stone People. Among the Sea People, the males do the cooking."

"Really?" Anjr said. Surprise made her gray eyes open even wider. Before she could ask any of the questions that she obviously had, a shouted order jerked her head up. With a curt nod, she walked back to the front of the cart and soon, they were moving again.

If Ka Lem stretched his legs out and leaned back awkwardly, he could rest his shoulders against the supplies lashed to the head of the cart with thick rope. It wasn't very comfortable, particularly given how the cart rocked back and forth. It was still better than sitting up on his own all the time, or lying down.

He knew that Anjr was not his friend. She'd probably been assigned as the driver of his cart because she appeared so innocent. He was suspicious of her, and assumed that everything he said to her would be repeated to the head of the guards.

However, it appeared that the Bone People knew very little of the rest of the world. And he'd been training to be a teacher. Perhaps, as he tried to educate her, he could bring her to his side.

Ka Lem wasn't optimistic about his chances. But a little hope was better than none.

Chapter Five

STONE

NOALANON CLOSED zir eyes and easily found the beacon of the stone ze'd "awoken." It was just ahead and to the left. Ze shifted zir path and led the most recently rescued group of prisoners toward "zir" rock, the feeling of the stone growing stronger as they moved closer.

Ze could tell that the Wind People were impatient with zir pace, despite their exhaustion and hunger. Ze was moving as fast as ze could, and ze no longer had zir skin hardened, but it would never be quick enough for the Wind People.

However, neither moon was full and it was extremely dark under the trees. Noalanon was the only one in the group who could actually see where they were going, as well as feel it.

When they were close enough, Noalanon gave a hooted cry, three times, as a signal to those waiting for them in the camp. Suddenly, a bright fire shone in the distance. The rescued Wind People rushed around zir, greeted by those waiting in camp with warm blankets and stew.

After many tears and rejoicing, Noalanon left the rescued Wind People in the hands of their own, who would take good care of them. Ze went over to check on Hirshamin the builder, one of the first Stone People they'd rescued.

Hirshamin had insisted on staying in the rescue camp rather than returning home immediately. Noalanon was never certain why. Hirshamin's muscular build seemed to have shrunken, and Noalanon had urged zir to eat as many minerals as ze could manage. Hirshamin still spent a lot of time motionless, staring out across the distance, looking back toward the Stone People's land.

"I did it," Hirshamin said as Noalanon drew closer. "I woke one of the mineral containers." Ze held up a stone container. While Noalanon had been drawn to a container that looked very similar to zir own skin—light gray, like dry river rock, with white lines running through it—Hirshamin's container was alabaster white marble, while Hirshamin zirself was dark, almost coal colored.

Noalanon would check again in the morning, but it seemed to zir that Hirshamin was finally back to normal. Ze had also finally rebraided zir black hair into intricate plaits along the side of zir head. Ze gave Noalanon a broad smile.

"I'm so happy that you were able to waken one of them!" Noalanon said. Ze hadn't been able to waken a second container, and the stones in the land of the Wind People all appeared to ignore zir.

"It…it was difficult." Hirshamin fell back into zir habit of long silences between zir words. Ze had only started taking such long pauses after ze had been captured by the Bone People. "But once I did the first one, the others were easy."

Ze indicated the pile of stones that Noalanon now saw sitting beside Hirshamin.

"Wait—you woke all those?" Noalanon asked, surprised.

"In a manner of speaking, yes," Hirshamin said, nodding. "I'm a builder," ze explained after a bit. "I should be able to work with any stone, anywhere."

"That makes sense," Noalanon said. Hirshamin could form stones into shapes without using any tools, sculpting the rock just with zir hands and magic.

"Now, the next question is, can *you* feel those stones?" Hirshamin said, turning and peering hard at zir.

Noalanon contained zir sigh. Ze was tired after the rescue that evening. It was very late, and ze needed to sleep.

However, ze also felt the need to encourage Hirshamin, who appeared to finally be doing something other than just sitting.

"I'll try," Noalanon said after a moment. "But I'm not very fresh right now."

"We should wait until the morning, then," Hirshamin replied immediately.

"No," Noalanon said. "I'll try it now anyway. Just…if I'm not successful, we can try again in the morning."

"All right," Hirshamin said.

Noalanon closed zir eyes and reached out with zir senses. It was easy for zir to pinpoint the stone container that ze'd already awakened. It still sat on the back of the cart, to the right, beyond the group of Wind People.

After a few moments, Noalanon opened zir eyes and turned zir head, deliberately facing the pile of rocks that Hirshamin had awoken before closing zir eyes again.

Could ze feel them? Was there anything there in front of zir? Ze often likened her awakened rock to a beacon, a shining light in the darkness.

There may, *may* have been something of a warm glow coming from the pile of rocks. However, it was just as likely to have been zir imagination, as when ze turned zir head away, then looked back again, ze couldn't feel anything at all.

"I'm sorry," Noalanon said when ze opened zir eyes again. "I can't feel—"

"You reached for your own rock first, right?" Hirshamin

said, peering at zir as if zir was a particularly intricate wall of stone that Hirshamin had to disassemble.

"I did," Noalanon said.

"Of course! I'm an idiot!" Hirshamin said. Ze raced off, moving very quickly for a Stone Person. He reappeared a few moments later, cradling the stone container that Noalanon had awoken very carefully in zir large hands, as if holding a tiny infant.

Then Hirshamin sat again and stared at the container, as if trying to decipher all its secrets through sheer stubbornness.

"Do you want me to try again?" Noalanon asked after a few long moments of silence.

"What?" Hirshamin said. Ze glanced up blankly. "Oh! I'm sorry. No. Not yet. Let me do some more work. You go rest."

Noalanon blinked, surprised. Obviously, the builder had some sort of idea. Could ze link Noalanon's rock with zir own?

Hirshamin ignored Noalanon as ze stood up. For a moment, ze swayed. Goodness, ze was tired. They had performed raids every other night for a week now. There were only a few people who were still missing. Scouts had already located another of the Bone People's camps and most of the rest of the prisoners.

However, there was still the one raid that had gone horribly wrong, when Daleki had been captured and Ka Lem had stayed behind, remaining a prisoner. Despite going back the following night, Noalanon hadn't been able to find the camp again. No one had. The Bone People had taken her two friends and disappeared.

The king of the Bone People—King Einar—had also disappeared. Had he just gone back to the homeland of the Bone People? No one knew.

Noalanon went to the cart that held the Stone People's bedding, grabbing zir bedroll, then took it out into the middle of the field to sleep. The cold didn't bother zir, and ze liked to see the stars at night.

After Noalanon had spread out zir blankets and laid down, ze expected to go directly to sleep. Instead, ze lay there with zir eyes open, exhaustion washing over zir but not dragging zir into the depths yet.

It took Noalanon a while to figure out that the reason ze wasn't sleeping: Something kept tugging at zir. Ze whispered a few words to zir mate Jolapen, then smiled at the warmth that immediately filled zir. Even across this much distance, ze still felt connected to Jolapen, able to share emotion and love if not actual words.

Noalanon had always thought that what some called a bedrock connection between a couple was romantic nonsense. Ze hadn't believed it to be possible.

Yet, even over this distance, Noalanon felt that connected to zir partner.

Slowly, sleep tugged Noalanon down and ze dreamed of being warm and safe, cuddled around Jolapen, sharing warmth and skin and not a cold, uncertain future.

WHEN THEY'D FIRST STARTED, Gan Ou and the others had insisted on going on a rescue mission every night. However, after just one they'd discovered that not only did the rescuers need their rest, those they rescued needed time to recover. The rescuers would stay at this camp for two or three days before dispersing the Wind People back to their homes. At least this group had been all Wind People. There was only one prison group that the scouts had found that still had Stone People.

Plus the group who'd taken Daleki.

After the first raid, the wall of smoke the Bone People hid behind had drawn back to the plain instead of being mingled with the forest. Three days later, the wall started marching forward again. It appeared to move slowly, about a half-day's walk every day. The rescuers had had to move their camp twice to stay ahead of its path.

How were the Bone People making the wall move? How was the wall powered? Everyone agreed that it was magic. But generated by who? By what?

And most important of all, how did the other Peoples stop it?

In the morning, Noalanon was very happy that they weren't on the move that day. Ze had slept well and felt rested, but still, there was something draining about being in this land. Ze couldn't wait to get back to the land of the Stone People, to feel as though the very ground itself supported zir.

The dawn came gray, cloudy, and cold. Noalanon raised zir own internal body temperature. There were plenty of blankets and warm furs for the rescued Wind People.

First thing that morning, one of the priestesses of the Wind People took all the former prisoners to a nearby stream, performing a purification ceremony. Noalanon hadn't understood it, as ze hadn't felt the darkness of the Bone People pour into zir soul. But all the Stone People who'd been prisoners had. They performed their own ceremony, standing naked in an open space and spiking their internal temperature until their skin glowed red, burning out the infection.

Noalanon wasn't convinced that either purification ceremony actually did any good. Most of the Wind People remained docile afterward, which was never a word Noalanon had ever used to describe Wind People before. Was that just an after effect of having been prisoners? Or were they still infected? Would it be easy for the Bone People to corrupt them again, and get the Wind People to turn against their own?

Ze didn't like to think of what would happen if the Stone People remained corrupted. They could do so much damage.

After eating a few minerals to regain zir strength, as well as heating up some water near to boiling before drinking it out of a stone mug, Noalanon went to find Hirshamin.

"Ah, good, you're awake," Hirshamin said cheerfully as Noalanon came up to greet zir.

Noalanon peered closely at the builder. Ze seemed to be doing much better that morning than since ze'd been rescued. Zir dark skin looked clear, as did zir blue eyes. Though Noalanon couldn't say for certain, ze would guess that Hirshamin's shoulders had broadened back to their original width as well.

"Now, hold this," Hirshamin said, handing Noalanon zir stone container. "Can you still feel it?"

Noalanon nodded slowly. "It isn't as strong," ze said after a moment. "It's as if the light has dimmed, like a lamp that now has a shade on it."

"Interesting," Hirshamin said. Ze reached out and touched the stone with one chubby finger. "And now?"

"Brighter," Noalanon said. "What did you do?"

"I can also now feel that stone," Hirshamin said. "I've put my name on it, while keeping yours there too."

"What do you mean?" Noalanon said.

"You told me that you put an awareness in the stone, right?" Hirshamin said. At zir nod, ze continued. "You kept talking about 'wakening' the rocks. That never felt right to me. These stones aren't aware. Not like the rocks back in our land."

Noalanon nodded, though ze didn't really understand.

"Instead of trying to awaken a stone, I pressed myself against it. I embossed my name on each one."

At Noalanon's confused expression, Hirshamin picked up one of the rocks from the pile beside zir. "Here," ze said, handing it to Noalanon. "Look at this."

Noalanon turned the rock over in zir hand. It was about six inches wide and only a few inches thick, rounded like a cylinder. Wind People ate a tuber that had this shape…a potato, ze thought it was called. The rock was a light brown gray in color, with dimples carved into it.

When ze rotated the rock, ze came to a spot that felt warmer than the rest. Ze used a single finger to trace it. It did, in fact, feel as though something was embossed on the spot, something ze couldn't see and could only barely feel.

"That's the spot exactly," Hirshamin said excitedly. "Now, the question is, can you find my name? Without touching it?"

Noalanon handed the rock back to Hirshamin and closed zir eyes, pushing out with zir senses. At first, it was just that warm spot, immediately in front of zir. But that wasn't enough. Ze knew that ze wouldn't be able to find it again at any distance.

So what did it mean to place your name on a rock? Had Hirshamin claimed these rocks to some extent? Made them more like their homeland? More supportive?

Noalanon deliberately turned zir away, setting zir face toward the land of the Stone People. It was funny how ze always knew exactly which direction that lay. Or perhaps what ze felt was the sacred mountain. Ze wouldn't know for certain until ze returned.

Then ze turned zir head back toward Hirshamin and sought that same feeling.

There. That warmth. It was stronger now.

Noalanon blindly reached out and put a single finger on

the stone that Hirshamin held. Ze could feel the mark much more strongly, and yes, it was Hirshamin's name.

Ze had the feeling, however, that it being Hirshamin's name wasn't as important as the fact that it was the name of a Stone Person, one of Noalanon's kind. It made the rock special in a way that ze could now track easily.

Finally, Noalanon opened zir eyes and looked back at Hirshamin.

"You did it!" Hirshamin said proudly. "You found the mark."

"Yes," Noalanon said, nodding. "I know these rocks. Can find them from a distance. Although," ze paused, thinking, "I can find my own rock at a greater distance. It also feels…different."

Hirshamin handed Noalanon's stone container back to zir. "What you did with this one, awakening it, means it belongs to you and no one else. I can feel it, but I'll never be able to form a strong connection to it. While with these," Hirshamin paused and gestured toward the pile sitting next to zir feet, "all Stone People should be able to sense."

"I see," Noalanon said. And ze did. Ze had felt the same. "Have I ruined this?" Noalanon asked, looking at the stone container.

"No, no! Not at all!" Hirshamin said. "What you did is much more difficult. And I believe, if the old legends are true, that that stone will one day be able to talk with you, particularly back in our lands."

Noalanon blinked, surprised. "Really?"

"Really," Hirshamin said. "It's the difference between awakening a stone and merely marking it. These stones," ze continued, gesturing at the pile next to zir feet, "will lose their power after a few years. The mark will be worn off. For now, they can act as beacons."

"For what?" Noalanon said, wary of the hard expression that Hirshamin's face suddenly held.

"For the rest of our people," Hirshamin said. "As they leave our lands to attack the Bone People."

NOALANON SAT at the edge of the meadow with zir back turned toward the camp, facing the direction of the land of the Stone People. The rain gently pattered on zir head, and ze blinked away the drops now and again. Ze sat on solid stone, trying to draw what comfort ze could from it. Tears lay at the back of zir throat, as well as bitter anger.

Ze had come on this journey because of a great injustice—the Bone People coming into the land of the Wind People. As well as the death of all the elk.

Ze had also known that a war was brewing. Particularly after being attacked by the Bone People the first time ze had gone through the wall.

However, what did it mean for all of the Stone People to go to war? Zir people never really fought, not even mock games like the Wind People did. Did it mean killing all the Bone People in order to drive them back? What would it take to stop them?

Ze knew that the answer to that actually lay in what was driving them. Ze had listened to more than one Wind Person talk about how the Bone People were on a holy mission, to bring word of their god Valtyr to the rest of the world.

Noalanon suspected that was just a cover story. No, the Bone People had something else they needed, something else that was driving them out of their territory and into the rest of the world. What did the Wind People have that the Bone People needed? Or was their final target the Wind People's territory? Did they actually have something else in mind? Was their final destination the Stone People, or the sea?

Gan Ou came up silently and sat down on the ground beside Noalanon. The rain soaked the ground. The Wind People whirled around behind them, flitting from one place to another. Noalanon had noticed that about the prisoners—since they'd been forced to be immobile when in captivity, they moved a lot when they were first free, never able to sit in one place for long, at least for a few days.

The old Wind Person beside Noalanon understood stillness. She didn't always practice it, but she could achieve it better than any of the others. So Noalanon suffered Gan Ou's presence that afternoon, even though ze really wanted to be left alone.

"It's the whys, ain't it?" Gan Ou asked after a blissful, quiet time. "Those are what keep you up at night."

Noalanon nodded. None of them had enough information about the Bone People, what they were doing, or why.

"You know what we're going to have to do, right?" Gan Ou said after allowing a decent amount of silence to fall between them.

"No," Noalanon said. She knew what Hirshamin thought they needed to do, but she had no idea what the Wind People thought was appropriate.

"We're going to need to capture one of them," Gan Ou said quietly. "So we can learn more."

"That will make us just as bad as they are," Noalanon pointed out.

"We won't treat them badly," Gan Ou assured zir. "But it's the only way to learn about their plans."

"And what if the Bone Person refuses to speak? Will you resort to torture?" Noalanon said, bitterness filling her mouth.

Gan Ou looked shocked at the question. Then she paused, considering it.

Noalanon didn't like how the old person's chin came up, how stubborn the Wind Person beside zir grew. "Only if it becomes necessary."

Noalanon gave a laugh that sounded as bitter as ze felt. "It will become necessary. Sooner than you can imagine."

Gan Ou sighed. "I'm afraid you're probably right."

Silence swam between them again, only now it was tense and deeply sad.

"Hirshamin is talking about leading a group of Stone People into the lands of the Bone People, to do battle with them," Gan Ou eventually said.

"I know," Noalanon said. "Ze's made a bunch of beacon rocks, so the Stone People can find their way through the lands of the Wind People."

Ze wasn't exactly sure how they would work, but they would form a good trail that only the Stone People would know was there. The Wind People couldn't distinguish between a rock that Hirshamin had put zir name on and one that ze hadn't.

Gan Ou sighed. "I'm not a teacher," she said after a bit. "And I never paid that much attention to the old myths and legends. They never seemed relevant, not to an impatient teenager."

That actually brought a smile to Noalanon, despite the cold and the wet of the morning, as well as the frightening future awaiting them.

"However, I believe that all the Peoples have tales of heroes who could do fantastic, magical things," Gan Ou said. "I thought they were just stories."

Noalanon nodded, curious about where the old Wind Person was going. She would never be allowed to be an elder for her people—she'd been banished for accidently killing someone in her youth, and some would never forgive her for it, would never trust her. However, Gan Ou had developed stillness while in the land of the Stone People. She thought deeply. It was a trait that Noalanon had come to admire.

"It appears that those hero tales weren't just stories. They were true. We have some, possibly all, of those abilities, as well as others."

Again Gan Ou paused.

Noalanon felt a shiver cross zir shoulders. Ze remembered Ka Lem asking if now was the time when they discovered just how many of those old myths were true.

"Why did we forget these abilities?" Gan Ou asked. "Why did we lose that power? What happened?"

Noalanon blinked, surprised. Ze hadn't taken zir own questions far enough, ze could tell.

"It's like that magic I still feel inside of me," Gan Ou said, her frustration making the words more of a growl. "I *know* I'm supposed to be able to call up the wind. We're named after the wind, not the animals we become. But that knowledge is lost to us, just like the form of the horses."

"I don't know what happened," Noalanon said slowly. "The Stone People keep better archives than the other peoples. I don't know if we'll find any clues there as to what happened in the past."

Gan Ou nodded. "The Sea People believe that we live in the third age, that there were two ages of people before ours. I don't think they're right—or rather, that it happened as they think it did. But I am starting to wonder about our ancestors. What battles did they have to fight? And did they forget their powers on purpose because they grew too mighty and too terrible?"

Long after Gan Ou had left, Noalanon sat brooding over the old Wind Person's words.

Had something so terrible occurred in the past that all

the people agreed to just let those deeds fade? Had there been a previous encounter with the Bone People? A war so awful it was better to forget it, to let it fade away rather than remember it?

Noalanon knew that the nature of zir people would be to let go, particularly if the memory had no practical value.

And no matter what anyone else might argue, war, at its heart, was immensely impractical.

NOALANON WAITED with the other rescuers in the darkness. Ahead of them lay the encampment of the Bone People, where the last of the prisoners were being held. Scouts were creeping around the edges of the camp to make sure that the layout was identical to every other camp that the Bone People had set up.

Clouds covered the night sky, hiding both moons as well as the stars. Earlier that evening, a fine dusting of snow had covered the broad plain. The air felt crisp, though it was still burdened with the strong smell of smoke.

The rescuers waited north and east of the camp, hiding behind the wooden carts that the Bone People would hook up to the elk in the morning. The chain that connected the elk together occasionally clanged as the dead animals shuffled their feet.

If the camp had been set up like the others, the prisoners would be laid out in a line in front of the elk, going north-south. While some of the smaller tents had their own fires, the main bonfire for the camp that everyone shared sat directly in the center of the camp. Guards and their tents filled the south side in an arc. Cooking tents, and the tents of those traveling with the group, primarily females, curved around the western side.

Noalanon would have thought that after the first few raids that the Bone People would change how they positioned their camp. They didn't, however. Was there some reason why everyone always set up their tents in the exact same locations every time they stopped? Did they have a strict hierarchy? Was it religious?

The Wind People gathered around Noalanon waited silently. It had surprised zir just how quiet the Wind People could be. Then again, they were great hunters. They just never applied that skill to other times of their lives.

It gave zir insight into how ze could better teach the students who came to Killapany to learn about the Stone People.

If ze could ever get home, if ze would ever go back to something as mundane as teaching again.

Je Long—the Wind Person crouched closest to Noalanon —reached out and touched zir back.

Noalanon understood the signal and stood. Only once had Noalanon been able to hear the words spoken on the wind that the Wind People shared. However, those words had also been directed at zir by one of the prisoners, trying to warn zir of the nearby traps.

The touch on zir back meant that the camp was set up identically, the guards were out on the perimeter guarding, and they should start the raid. If Je Long had touched zir knee or zir shoulder, they would either wait or withdraw, respectively.

Noalanon slowly walked forward, past the roughly made carts, around the staring elk. Ze felt the heat of their eyes on zir, but the elk didn't make a sound.

They filled zir with dread.

Noalanon made zir way to the northern-most end of the chain connecting the prisoners together, while Yunaki went to the other end. Hirshamin waited in the darkness, ready to aid either of them if necessary. It was Hirshamin's first rescue. Noalanon had tried to talk zir into staying behind in the camp, but ze had insisted on coming.

The chain for the prisoners was connected to a huge iron anchor, as always. Noalanon wished once more that they had time for zir to study the anchor more closely. It looked like a two-foot square box that had the edges blunted. Ze had run zir hands across one once, and had been surprised to find delicate carvings across all the faces ze could reach.

Was it solid metal? Ze suspected that it had to be hollow in order for the Bone People to be able to lift it. Or was there something inside of it? Did it have an opening?

Noalanon didn't have time to answer all of zir questions. Instead, ze knelt down and placed zir hands on the cold iron links that connected the prisoners to the anchor.

The chain was always cold to the touch. Noalanon suspected that was a result of the magic running through the iron.

Noalanon focused on zir hands. While zir internal core temperature remained about the same, ze changed the temperature of zir hands, making them freezing cold. It took a lot of concentration to freeze just zir hands and not the rest of zir body.

The trick worked as it always had. Frost crystals crept across the iron that stuck out from under zir palms.

When Noalanon judged the iron to be sufficiently cold, ze let go of the link. Then, with all of zir considerable strength, ze smashed zir palm against the chain. The super-chilled iron shattered with a quiet tinkle.

Noalanon immediately stood back up and scanned the area for guards. The sound of the iron cracking generally brought people to the vicinity. No one came running up, though.

The Wind People stretched out in a line began changing

shapes, shrinking themselves down so they could slip out of the iron shackles around their ankles. It always went more slowly than Noalanon would have liked. However, the longer that the Wind People had been forced to stay in their Wind Person shape, the longer it took for them to find an animal form to change into.

Except for one. A person toward the center of the group. They stood up and tugged at the chain, trying to pull it out from between their feet.

Before Noalanon could go to their aid, the guards attacked.

Arrows flew through the air, striking many of the Wind People in mid-transformation.

Noalanon startled at the shrieks of anguish.

What was happening? Before now, the guards always started with their nets. They wanted to recapture the Wind People, not kill them. It wasn't until the end of any raid that the guards got desperate enough to use arrows or javelins.

"Help me!" came a strange, lilting voice.

Noalanon rushed toward the sound, not realizing until ze approached that the person who'd stood up, who still had their ankles encased in shackles, was a Bone Person.

What was a Bone Person doing chained up to the rest of the Wind People? Why would they do that to one of their own?

Noalanon didn't have time for questions, though. "Crouch down!" ze ordered.

The Bone Person looked startled, but complied.

Noalanon forced the Bone Person down further, protecting their body from the rain of arrows with zir own. Then ze reached over and broke the chain on one side of the shackles, yanking it through the other side, freeing the Person from the chain, though they'd have to wear the shackles for a while.

All around Noalanon, ze heard the sounds of battle, the yelps and rough growls of the Wind People attacking the guards, the screams that indicated yet another death, the foul smell of blood and gore carried on the wind.

The Bone Person still hiding beneath Noalanon was shaking. Fear? Or something else? They had a peculiar odor to them, similar to the smoky scent of ashes.

"Save me," the Bone Person said softly.

Their words had a lilting quality to them, though their tone was harsh. Noalanon glanced at the Person. They had a halo of golden hair. Their face was pale, with a huge nose and wideset dark eyes. Thin cruel lips, high cheekbones, and a wide mouth were all that ze had time to see.

"Come with me," Noalanon said, making up zir mind.

Gan Ou and the others had talked of kidnapping one of the guards.

A willing prisoners would be a much better source of information than a hostile hostage.

Noalanon grabbed hold of the Bone Person's forearm, wrapping zir fingers across their skin tightly. While the Bone Person had muscles, Noalanon knew that they couldn't match zir strength. "This way," ze said.

Instead of going south, where the rest of the Wind People and the few they'd managed to rescue had gone, Noalanon went north, past the elk and the carts. Ze would rendezvous with the rest of the rescue team close to the wall. The scouts would reconnect them before ze tried to go through the wall on zir own.

The Bone Person followed along meekly, though the elk all stared at them as they passed, their red hot gaze blasting Noalanon's body.

Then they passed beyond the camp, out onto the quiet plane. The sound of the fight faded in the distance. Noalanon turned west, or at least roughly west. Ze still knew the direction of the land of the Stone People, and so walked that way.

"Hurry!" the Bone Person said nervously looking over their shoulder.

Noalanon shrugged. Ze was moving as fast as ze could with zir skin hardened.

The Bone Person tried to break away, but couldn't free themselves from Noalanon's grip.

"You're coming with me," ze said simply as ze kept walking.

"Can't you go any faster?" the Bone Person asked, obviously impatient.

"No," Noalanon said. Ze didn't want to give the Bone Person any more information than that. They trudged together in silence. Another scream cut through the air but Noalanon kept up zir steady pace.

The Bone Person kept looking over their shoulder, toward the camp. "They're not following us," they remarked after a moment.

"No, they went after the larger group," Noalanon said.

"Clever," the Bone Person said after a moment, nodding their approval. "Thank you," they added after another few long moments of silence.

"You're welcome," Noalanon said. When ze judged that they were far enough away, ze finally gave into zir curiosity. "Who are you? Why were you confined with the others?"

"My name is Forni," the Bone Person said. "I tried...I tried to help the prisoners escape."

"Why would you do that?" Noalanon asked, surprised. It was the first time ze had ever heard of a Bone Person trying to help the Wind People. None of the others they'd rescued had ever told of such a tale.

Forni sighed. "They just...they looked so miserable all the time. It wasn't right."

Noalanon shook zir head. "But none of the other Bone People even consider the Wind People, well, people. Worthy of rescue. Why do you think so differently than the others?"

"My mother was a slave," Forni said plainly.

"A what?"

Forni shot Noalanon a look that ze couldn't interpret. "A slave. Someone who is owned by their master, and must always do what they're told."

Noalanon couldn't contain zir gasp. "Slave?" ze asked, wanting to make sure that ze had the word correct.

Forni nodded. "Yes. But she was a very wise female. Worthy of respect. Eventually her master saw that, and freed me."

"And you didn't like seeing others being made into slave?" Noalanon said.

"Slaves. Yes. They needed to be freed, like me," Forni said.

"You will have to tell us all about it later," Noalanon said when a breeze suddenly circled zir. Ze didn't hear any words carried on the wind, but ze knew that a Wind Person was close, either a scout or one of the rescue party.

That the Bone People kept slaves didn't really surprise Noalanon. They had to treat some portion of their population bad, otherwise they wouldn't have such shackles near at hand.

Had they come to the lands of the Wind People in order to turn them into slaves? Was that the real reason for their invasion?

Noalanon didn't know, but at least for the first time, felt as if ze might find some answers.

Chapter Six

——————————

SEA

THE NIGHT AFTER MAYLETH DIED, Ajooless put her foot down, both literally and metaphorically. "You must give us more water," she insisted to Helge, the high priest of the Bone People who had captured them. "We require more than you or anyone else."

Helge glared at her. His frizzy yellow hair had tendrils of gray running through it, and his brown eyes had flecks of green and gold in them. Lines ran down his face, making him look more like an old Wind Person. All this, plus his position, led Ajooless to assume he was the eldest in the group of Bone People who'd taken them prisoner.

Despite his age, he still refused to listen to her and insisted on doing things the way the Bone People did. He reminded her of her parents in that respect, stubborn and set in his ways instead of learning to be wise as he gained years.

Helge wore an off-white shirt that covered him from neck to wrist, long black pants that went to his ankles, as well as a beautifully embossed leather belt wider than Ajooless' palm. No one else in the group of ten Bone People had as fancy of a belt.

"If you don't give us more water, every day, all of us will die," Ajooless said. As far as she could tell, it was the truth. It had been their primary concern about taking the southern route across the mountains to the land of the Wind People. They always had to find water along the way.

Helge stayed silent, his arms crossed over his chest, looking to the side. Ajooless waited patiently in front of him. She stood tall and proud, at least a head taller than the priest. Her sleeveless light-green shirt and long, darker-green pants were covered in dirt from being forced to sleep on the ground instead of her bedroll. Her skin was dry and flaky from not bathing, and had also taken on a gray pallor, instead of being milky blue. Though she had no mirror in which to see herself, she suspected that the bony ridge that ran across the top of her head had grown more prominent, as it had in the other prisoners.

The Sea People were all exhausted, worn out by the hard travel and the constant fear of what the Bone People would do to them next. The scouts had come upon Ajooless and her group much more quickly than anticipated. The dark miasma that Helge commanded took Ajooless' will from her and the others.

Until Ajooless got her feet wet, and she was able to resist.

Some of the others speculated that the magic Helge had only worked on their land form, that their sea form was immune. Either that, or Helge didn't realize just how different the two forms were and so wasn't trying to control both at the same time.

At least most of the Sea People had managed to escape from Helge and his group. The first time they'd come across a deep enough river, the Sea People had slipped away into the water, transforming and swimming away quickly.

Only four of the Sea People had remained in captivity. Three, now that Mayleth had died.

The Bone People hadn't allowed Ajooless or the others near another body of water. Which was smart, as the Sea People would have escaped given a chance. That was the strict instruction that Ajooless had given to each and every person: escape as quickly as they could.

However, the Sea People needed water. They would die without it.

"Fine," Helge finally said. His whole face looked puckered, as if he'd just tasted the bitterest seaweed tea. "You will have your water. Ingeborg!"

One of the females of the Bone People came scurrying up. They all seemed scared of Helge, which Ajooless could understand. He was a bully, petty and capricious. Not a true leader.

Ajooless thought fondly of Liseth, how she could get the regents with their strong personalities and their power to compromise and agree. Ajooless had never appreciated her mentor more than she did now.

Ingeborg was one of the youngest in the group of Bone People, at least as far as Ajooless could tell. Round pink cheeks sat high on her pale face. Her hair was a mousy brown color, and frizzed around her face under her broad straw hat. The belt she wore was the least fancy of any of the Bone People, made of stiffened off-white cloth with no decorations or bands of color. Many pouches hung from the belt. Like the rest of the Bone People, she was completely covered up. Her clothing always looked uncomfortable. Ajooless wasn't certain if it was just so harshly spun or badly made.

"Give the prisoners a second flask of water. Tonight," Helge said, glaring at Ajooless.

Ajooless looked down on the priest, then shook her head. She sat down on the ground.

She nearly laughed at the expression of disbelief on both Ingeborg's and Helge's faces.

"No," Ajooless said. "Mayleth died last night because we didn't have enough water. We will not take another step without more water."

She knew that Helge could organize the rest of the Bone People, make them pick up the Sea People one by one and put them onto the back of one of the carts and carry them off. They'd done it before. Particularly after Helge poured his filth out onto them, made them more compliant.

However, no matter how much Helge directed the will of the Sea People, he couldn't make them do something that would cause them to physically harm themselves. For example, he couldn't direct them all to go march off the edge of a cliff and kill themselves.

Nor could he force them to continue without water. One by one, they'd all lie down and die.

Helge pressed his lips together so tightly that his already white skin turned pale around his mouth. A vein appeared to be throbbing under the pale skin of his temple.

He transferred his mighty anger to Ingeborg. "Get them water," he ordered. "And no gossiping with anyone else. Be quick about it."

The female raced away, her head bowed. Helge's glare followed her as she moved quickly through the camp.

Ajooless suddenly grasped why Helge was so very, very angry at her insubordination.

He'd had to compromise in front of one of the other Bone People, to show his weakness.

Ingeborg probably was correct to be afraid of him, as he'd likely take out his anger on her.

That was no concern of Ajooless. She had to keep focused on staying alive, as well as on doing the best she could for the two other remaining Sea People.

On the other hand, Liseth had taught Ajooless to use

anything and everything at hand when it came to diplomacy, to the art of persuasion.

Could Ajooless perhaps use Ingeborg to help her people?

AJOOLESS TRUDGED along with the rest of the Sea People across the open plain. The winter grass had been weighed down by a late, heavy snow. Piles of it still lurked around the edges of the open fields, under the shade of the trees. But winter had lost its hold of the season, and in the clear areas, the wan sun had melted the snow back down to a short, spotty covering, with patches of new spring green showing through.

Birds boldly greeted them every morning, and the winds were much more playful. Nothing was blooming—not yet— but Ajooless found herself always trying to catch the scent of flowers on the air.

The Bone People and their prisoners had been traveling together for a few weeks now, possibly a month. It was difficult for Ajooless to keep track of the days sometimes.

Ajooless and the two other Sea People—Delayness and Patereth—talked when they could about how to escape. At least the snow did an adequate job of providing constant moisture for the Sea People. No matter how much filth Helge tried to pour over them, how he tried to drain their will, the constant wetting of their feet helped them stay in control.

They had no plan, other than to look for a way to escape. They couldn't run as fast as the Bone People. Their best chance was to dive into the water, any water.

Ajooless wasn't looking forward to what would happen to them once they left the snowy plains and arrived in a dryer area.

As far as she could tell, they were still traveling through the lands of the Wind People. The Bone People carefully avoided any of the Wind People's villages. When they traveled on roads, they'd frequently hidden when anyone approached.

Ajooless had thought about shouting out to the Wind People who passed them, but to what end? Helge would just pour his filth over them, capturing their will and their minds, forcing them to do whatever the Bone People said.

No, better that just her group stayed in the clutches of the Bone People.

She'd asked Ingeborg a few times where it was that they were going. The poor person had looked scared, as if a ghost were speaking. Helge had probably warned Ingeborg about talking with the prisoners.

Though Ajooless wasn't alone, she often felt as if she were. The other two Sea People were kept separated from her. They couldn't talk to each other easily. And more than once Ajooless had been slapped or punched when she'd tried.

(At least the Bone People had learned early that the Sea People didn't take any sort of physical punishment well. Their bones were more brittle. Which meant they were easily killed. Ajooless still mourned for the three they'd lost in the party just due to their initial encounter.)

Why were the Bone People so concerned about keeping the Sea People alive? It didn't make any sense to Ajooless and the others. What was their goal? Were they just to be put into a tank, like the fish at the market, for the other Bone People to gape at them?

Fortunately, it wasn't just the Sea People who delayed the Bone People. Their elk also didn't travel fast or well. They were immensely strong. Ajooless had marveled more than once how the elk could pull the four-wheeled cart they were lashed to over small hills, ignoring any rocks the cart rolled over. They moved mindlessly forward, nothing stopping them.

The snow melted under the gaze of the elk, leaving a steaming trail behind. Anyone could follow the group easily enough. Ajooless sometimes had dreams that hunters of her people were coming after her and the others, a team of elite Sea People who would come to their rescue.

Mostly, though, she left those silly, girlish dreams behind and focused instead on the day-to-day tasks of staying alive, keeping her people alive, as well as giving them what hope she could.

Ajooless and the other Sea People began coughing one morning, smelling smoke in the air. It wasn't from their fire, no, it was carried to them on the wind. The Bone People all seemed to be happier that day, a spring in their step.

That night, after they'd formed camp (always in the exact same layout of tents) Ajooless asked Ingeborg why everyone seemed so happy.

For the first time, the Bone Person answered Ajooless. "We are closer to our own territory. Soon we'll be leaving the accursed lands." She dropped off the flask of water for Ajooless and scurried away, taking flasks over to the other Sea People.

Ajooless let the comment slide. She'd heard variations on the theme every night when Helge came to preach over them, his filth washing over them, making them docile. None of the Sea People would try to escape at night because of his preaching. However, in the morning, with their ration of water, they'd all "wake up."

Helge believed that the Sea People were naturally resilient to his magic. He also didn't have the strength or power to preach over them in the mornings as well as in the evenings. There seemed to be a limit, and he only had the power once a day.

The Bone People had never seemed to figure out that water washed their control away. The Sea People didn't need much—just a few drops on their skin and the magic would dissolve. Water applied to the Sea People's feet was most effective, though water dripped anywhere on their skin worked.

"Where are we going in the lands of the Bone People?" Ajooless asked when Ingeborg came back to collect the flask.

"Melefels, the capital," Ingeborg said. "I've never been there before," she added shyly. Then she started. She appeared to suddenly realize that she was actually talking to one of the Sea People. She snatched the water flask out of Ajooless' hand and raced away.

The capital city of the Bone People? What devilry awaited them there? Ajooless had heard the Bone People talk of their king. Were the Sea People being brought to meet him? But why? They were slaves—another new term that Ajooless had learned. They were nothing. Filth.

Ajooless prayed to Ishkra for her wisdom, to help her see a path out of the darkness that appeared to be all around them.

The goddess, however, never answered.

<hr>

DELAYNESS, Patereth, and Ajooless spent time every night searching the aquifers deep under the ground, seeking to connect where they were to the sea. There weren't any rivers that ran across the land—they all appeared to run north and south.

Ajooless remembered finding the headwaters of the Bone People once. When she focused, she could find them again, and knew they lay ahead of them, a bit to the north of their current location. If she had to guess, she'd say that the capital of the Bone People lay somewhere between the capitals of the Sea People to the south and the Wind People to the north.

Heavy rains started, indicating the start of spring. The Bone People looked miserable and huddled in their tents at night. They wove large straw hats to keep both the sun and the water off of them during the day. But their clothing had to be incredibly soggy and wet. Ajooless almost felt sorry for them. Particularly since the Sea People's clothing was specifically woven to be worn on both the land as well as underwater. They welcomed the rain like spring flowers, washing their skin, refreshing their spirits.

The rains made it easier to find networks of small creeks that connected one to another, always seeking a path going east and west.

However, if Ajooless could find the headwaters of the Bone People, so could some of the other Sea People. They had to act quickly, though. Once spring ended and the waters started drying up, the line would be broken.

What was happening back in Shiboleth and its sister water city, Sillboden? Had Liseth heeded Ajooless' warnings? Had most of the Sea People vacated the land and gone to the sea?

For two more days after the initial scent of smoke had wafted in on the winds, as the group traveled, the smell of smoke grew thicker. Ajooless found herself frequently breathless. Without her even asking, Helge increased the amount of water the Sea People got every day. He was probably just tired of listening to them constantly coughing.

Finally, they broke out of a copse of trees and saw it. The wall. The mysterious barrier that Ajooless and the others had merely heard of.

The wall rose all the way up into the gray sky and appeared to mingle with the clouds up there. Mists swam through the fog, like schools of minnows close to the shore.

The scent of the smoke made Ajooless cough harder. She shivered, certain that the temperature had just dropped.

What was this thing? Why had the Bone People erected it? How could they maintain it?

For the first time in a long while, Ajooless felt truly afraid. The Bone People she'd met so far had been unimpressive, petty, their magic easily defeated with just a little water.

This, though, was a monument to much greater magic than Ajooless had ever conceived of. All of the people—Wind, Stone, and Sea—had small magic, nothing as large or as grand as this.

The group of Bone People stopped for a while in front of the wall, making preparations for going through it. They tied ropes onto the cart, as well as to the elk itself. Ajooless assumed the Bone People would hold onto the ropes and be guided through the mists.

Huh. So they created the wall, but it was hostile to them?

Ingeborg came over and took Ajooless' hand. She used a short bit of rope to tie their wrists together.

Ajooless nearly snickered. She knew, *knew* that she should be taking this seriously. She was so far away from her home. These people had captured her, held her prisoner now for weeks. Forced her to walk away from everything she knew and loved.

But the goddess was always depicted with a smile on her face. Ajooless's teachers had constantly scolded her for being irreverent at the most inappropriate times.

Still, something of her laughter probably slipped through, as Ingeborg finally asked, "What is it?"

"Part of the ceremony for marriage involves tying the couple's wrists together," Ajooless said. At least on land. She didn't add that for the sea ceremony, the couple's ankles were tied together.

Ingeborg gasped. "We had the same tradition," she whispered. "At least according to the old tales."

Ajooless smiled, adding another notch to her mental scorecard. Every time she managed to get Ingeborg to see the Sea People as People, and not as animals or merely slaves (a new word for her), was another chance that maybe, someday, the Bone People would let them go.

Or Ingeborg would see that it was wrong to keep them and help them escape.

"Now, you need to stay with me," Ingeborg said sternly as she gripped Anjooless's hand hard. "Or you'll get lost in the mist, and may never come out."

Ajooless nodded, though she wondered if it was possible to be permanently lost in a wall of fog. Particularly for one of her people.

While the Wind and Stone People had a great sense of direction when they were in their own lands, the Sea People always knew which direction water lay. And Ajooless had a good sense of where the sea was, even this far away, by following all the underwater streams.

Delayness and Patereth had clear instructions from Ajooless—they were to try to escape any time they thought they might have a chance.

Whereas Ajooless would stay behind and continue traveling with the Bone People. The others didn't like it, but they couldn't outvote her. She was still the representative of the temple, the priestess of their group.

Before they'd been captured, Ajooless had split their group into smaller fractions. Hycineth and the two other scouts had been instructed to follow the Bone People. Had they been following the group all along? Ajooless assumed so.

If Delayness and Patereth escaped while they were crossing the wall, Hycineth and the scouts could take care of them, get them back to the land of the Sea People.

While Ajooless could carry on to the capital of the Bone People and meet this king of theirs, to act as the representative for the Sea People.

Plus, she *had* to touch the headwaters of the Bone People. Carry the knowledge of where they lay back to her people, so that someone, somewhere, could *deal* with them.

The Bone People approached the wall with reverence and awe, like children coming to the main temple for the first time and being brought to the feet of the goddess. Ajooless was more curious than fearful, though the smell of smoke continued to choke her and make her cough.

However, the first lick of mist cleared her head.

The Bone People didn't realize that the wall, while composed of smoke, was held together with fog.

Ajooless felt something stirring deep in her soul as they walked, completely surrounded by water suspended in clouds. There was a way of talking to the mist, even corrupted as it was by smoke and the Bone People.

Could Ajooless take control of the fog? Make it swirl and do her bidding? Draw it up out of damp ground herself, then send it back again?

There was a kernel of truth to the images that suddenly filled her head, she knew. But she also knew that she wouldn't have time to pursue them. The edge of the wall drew near. She could feel it, like the border of a lake.

Ajooless didn't want to go back to the harsh dryness on the other side. She stopped, tugging hard on Ingeborg's hand as power filled her.

It occurred to Ajooless that all she had to do was to call out. She clicked her tongue and made a trilling noise, unlike any sound she'd ever made before.

The mists swirled around her, like a current of water.

Her hand and arm were suddenly jerked, hard, Ingeborg trying to get her moving again.

Ajooless took a stumbling step forward, while reaching back with her other hand, keeping it in the heart of the wall.

She trilled again.

The mist formed a hand and wrapped it around her outstretched one, giving her an anchor.

Ajooless knew that with time, she could learn more about the wall, how to form the mist, how to make it protect her.

She could even use it to sever the rope tying her to Ingeborg. Drown the frightened female, or possibly strangle her with ropes of fog.

However, that wasn't to be Ajooless' fate. Instead, she reluctantly let go of the hand of mist, let it fade back as she turned and took the last few steps, leaving behind the wonderful comfort of all that water hanging in the air.

They left the wall with a soft *pop*. To Ajooless, it felt like bobbing up out of the sea after having been swimming in the depths for a long while.

Ingeborg stared at her with huge eyes, her mouth moving but no words coming out.

People started shouting. Helge barged up to Ajooless. "Where are they? Where did the other prisoners go?"

Ajooless just smiled at him. He already knew. The Sea People had better control of the mists than the Bone People. They'd just escaped.

And apparently had killed the guards who they'd been tied to.

She felt elated that they'd followed the plan and had taken their chance, seeking freedom.

While Ajooless would continue her way toward knowledge.

THE BONE PEOPLE traveled quickly away from the wall of

mist, probably frightened that Ajooless could send it after them. They didn't set up camp until late that night, as evening approached.

After getting her ration of water and eating a little of the stew the Bone People seemed to exist on, she braced herself for Helge's approach.

However, he merely glared at her after making sure that she was bound to the cart, then walked to the campfire. He stood on the southern side, in the center of the camp.

The priest started chanting, a sing-song hymn that she couldn't catch all the words of. It appeared to be a plea to his god, Valtyr, to help him reach the darkness that was the firmament for all.

Dark clouds gathered in the air, swirling above the head of the priest. She'd seen him do this before, when he'd preached at her and the other Sea People, pouring out his corruption and stealing their will from them.

However, this time, the magic wasn't being directed at her or the others. Instead, Helge appeared to be ordering the clouds. He directed them with his hand, making them swirl faster. They took on weight, coalescing into a solid mass, like a storm cloud filled with hail. Sparks lit the interior of the darkness, as if he'd captured half a dozen angry fireflies in the interior of the cloud, or maybe hornets who could buzz as well as cast their own light.

The smell of smoke washed over Ajooless, thick and heavy, like green reeds being burnt, the ashes oily and black. She tried to breathe through it, not wanting to cough and remind the priest that she still sat there, observing him.

The swirling mass over Helge's head swelled. The blinking lights in the interior of it grew more frenzied. Helge used his hands to direct the darkness, first attempting to compress it down into a more compact form, then, suddenly flinging it outward.

Ajooless followed the darkness past the light of the campfire, across the gray clouds of the sky. It gained speed quickly, moving off…somewhere.

Why had Helge just done that? Was it a message to someone? Who would receive it? What would they do with it?

Ajooless had to admit that for the first time, Helge had impressed her. A smidge. He was still a self-righteous asshole and a petty bully. But it appeared that he had greater magic than she'd expected.

Helge now appeared exhausted. His pale face looked even whiter in the firelight. Dark hollows under his eyes made them seem even larger than usual, like black holes in his skull. His hands trembled as he pushed his hair back out of his face.

None of the other Bone People came to help their priest, though. Instead, he walked with slow, shuffling steps toward his own tent.

When Ajooless saw one of the guards perhaps an hour later, she realized that he, too, looked wan, as if he'd been running beside the cart all day instead of leisurely walking.

It took Ajooless only a few moments to put it all together.

Like Mayleth and Jukaless, and even Ajooless to a lesser extent, Helge was able to use the strength of the Bone People around him in order to do his great magic. It meant that at least some of the powers of the Bone People was similar to those of the Sea People.

Ajooless wished she could form her own dark cloud and send it flying off to Liseth and the others, carrying all the information she was gathering about the Bone People.

That had always been the one great flaw in her plan. Though it made sense for her to continue forward into the land of the Bone People, to find their home waters, how was she going to send that knowledge home? She'd tried reaching out and talking through the fish again, but she didn't have the power to do it on her own. She needed the strength of others to aid her.

Still, she was going to have to try.

Chapter Seven

WIND

GAN OU DIDN'T LIKE this Forni who Noalanon had rescued. Too many prisoners had died when they'd come to rescue this group, the Bone People changing their strategy this fateful time.

It felt like a trap. And oh how convenient that this Bone Person just happened to be a prisoner with the rest of them!

However, none of the others would listen to her. Particularly not when the three (merely three!) Wind People that they'd managed to rescue out of the dozen or so who'd been trapped all backed up his story.

Not that they'd seen him help anyone. He had been chained in with the prisoners for a few days, brought to the camp at the same time they'd been transferred over, from the camp they'd been staying in.

No one listened to Gan Ou, though. She wasn't one of the travel elders. She'd been busting her butt to rescue all the Wind People who'd been captured. Evidentially, that wasn't enough.

It would never be enough for some. Particularly Je Long,

who, it turned out, was related to Ru Jing, the elder who held a deep abiding grudge against her.

Gan Ou sat on the edge of the camp that morning, her back to the rest of the camp while she looked out over the dark trees that towered in front of her. They'd been at this camp for a few days now, waiting while the rescued Wind People recovered. They'd been held the longest, and everyone was still in shock from the violence of the encounter.

Why had the Bone People suddenly used arrows to kill the prisoners? Why hadn't they used their nets instead, trying to recapture everyone? Was it because this was the last group? Had they finally figured out that all their prisoners were gone?

The day was at least sunny, though cold. Winter had passed and spring was bearing down on them. The season wouldn't last long, though. Summer would come hard on its heels, this plain baking in the hot sun, the grass browning quickly. Water would be scarce, though rocks would be plentiful.

When Gan Ou looked around, coming out of her deep thoughts, she saw that Noalanon sat beside her. That was something that Gan Ou truly appreciated in the Stone People: they could move completely silently.

It had been useful for their raids. And would probably be even more useful in the coming war.

"What are your plans?" Gan Ou asked, not bothering with greetings or stupidly asking Noalanon about how zir day was going.

Noalanon gave her a smile. At least ze was used to the Wind People and their bluntness. It had been difficult sometimes, talking with the others. Particularly Hirshamin, who always appeared to be offended whenever anyone approached zir.

"I think that Hirshamin, Yunaki, and I will not be

stopping in Shan Yu, but instead, heading directly back to Killapany," Noalanon said slowly.

"Good," Gan Ou said. When Noalanon shot her a questioning look, she continued. "I want you safe," she explained. "The Bone People—they're all headed toward Shan Yu. There will be a big fight there. While the Stone People are awesome fighters, and we welcome their help, you've done enough."

"Have I?" Noalanon said.

The bitterness of the laugh ze gave surprised Gan Ou.

"There's still a huge injustice being done. And I'd promised not to go home until I'd seen it righted," Noalanon continued.

"This is bigger than just one person," Gan Ou pointed out reasonably. She, too, had done enough. More than enough. It was time for other people, younger people, to carry the torch of this war.

"I know," Noalanon said. "It's just that—I hate feeling as if my job is unfinished."

Gan Ou shrugged. "Maybe you need to redefine your work." That was what she felt she needed to do. She'd been a messenger for the elders. Had flown back and forth along the entire border of the Wind People's territory. She'd carried the news of the wall, been attacked by it. She'd rescued most of the people who'd been captured by the Bone People.

Surely that was enough?

Noalanon sighed. "I know you're right. I know that instead of going off on my own I need to go and consult with the leaders of my People. Talk to the council. Form a cohesive plan of attack, or defense. Something." Ze paused and gave Gan Ou a sly smile. "Yunaki has accused me more than once of being infected by the Wind People, of wanting to work by myself instead of as a group."

Gan Ou snorted in derision. "Next thing I know, you'll

be sprouting wings with the rest of us." Then she sobered. "It is good to be going home." She'd been doing her best out here with limited resources. It was time to return to Shan Yu, to find out what the rest of the plan was, how the Wind People were coping with the invasion of the Bone People.

She wouldn't allow herself to dwell on the possibility that there wouldn't be much for her to return to. No, the Wind People had had plenty of warning. They would have turned back the Bone People by now.

Noalanon nodded. Ze turned zir face away, looking out onto the woods ahead of them. Behind them, Gan Ou could hear the rest of the people in the camp. They went quietly about their business, making food, singing prayers of thanks for their rescue, with a few off to one side chanting while doing a shuffling dance.

She didn't know what Forni was doing. Didn't care. Didn't like him. He wasn't telling the truth, she just knew it. He wore a false skin that no one else seemed to sense.

"What about Ka Lem?" Noalanon finally asked quietly. "And Daleki?"

Gan Ou felt herself shrink down into herself.

She'd tried to rescue all the prisoners. Eighty-one Wind People had approached the wall the previous winter, just before the solstice. Fewer than forty people were returning. Gan Ou could account for all of those who were missing, either killed by the Bone People or else had taken their own lives, too degraded by whatever magic the Bone People had done to them to be willing to live.

Only one was missing, unaccounted for.

Ka Lem.

And Daleki, the one Stone Person who'd been trapped in a hole by the Bone People during one of the first rescues.

The scouts had never been able to find a camp of Bone People with prisoners that contained those two.

Where had they been taken to? Gan Ou couldn't assume that Ka Lem and Daleki had escaped. They were still back there, behind the wall, somewhere.

"I don't know what to do about Ka Lem," Gan Ou said after a bit. "Or Daleki." There had been some talk in the camp about trying to track them. But where had they gone?

One of the theories had been that for some reason, one of the camps of Bone People had turned away from invading the Wind People and were instead traveling back to their own homelands with the prisoners.

But why?

Either that, or the Bone People had killed Ka Lem as well as Daleki. That didn't make any sense, though. Why go to all the trouble to set a trap for one of the Stone People if they didn't want a prisoner?

Noalanon sighed.

Gan Ou heard both the frustration as well as anger that the Stone Person sitting beside her felt.

"There is a part of me that wants to go back to the land of the Bone People, to see if I can find Ka Lem and Daleki," Noalanon admitted. "Hirshamin and I have talked about it. We would leave a trail of rocks behind us that any of the Stone People could follow."

A touch of excitement—or maybe fear—stirred deep inside Gan Ou. "If you decided to do that, you may have help from the Wind People," she said. Not that she was considering it herself. No, her job was done, damn it!

Noalanon shook zir head. "The problem is that we're low on supplies. We may, *may* be able to track the Bone People for a month or so. But then we'd run out of minerals. We'd starve."

Gan Ou thought for a moment. "What if you start your journey and supplies were delivered to you? The Wind People can travel much faster than the Stone People. We might be able to supply you."

"That is true," Noalanon said slowly. "However, it's only my own People who could follow us. The Wind People wouldn't see the trail. Particularly if they were flying."

Gan Ou shrugged. "We could figure something out," she insisted stubbornly.

"I'll bring it up to Hirshamin," Noalanon promised.

The sound of a lilting voice carried on the wind. Gan Ou shuddered. It was that damned Forni.

"What are we going to do about him?" she asked.

Noalanon blinked at her, before asking, "Forni?"

"Yes. Him."

"You do not trust them—him," Noalanon said slowly. "I do not either. I know the other Wind People consider him harmless. None of the Bone People are harmless."

Relief washed over Gan Ou. "Thank you," she said softly. She hadn't realized how much it had hurt for none of the others to believe her. As well as pissed her off.

"Hirshamin actually proposed that we should take Forni with us, to Killapany," Noalanon said. "I wasn't sure I wanted them—him—any closer."

"But you're less susceptible to the magic of the Bone People," Gan Ou said excitedly. "It would be safer for you to travel with him."

"Safer does not mean safe," Noalanon said with a grimace. "We would watch him more carefully, though."

Gan Ou nodded. While she loved her own People, she also was aware that they weren't the most careful. Despite what had happened to them at the hands of the Bone People, the Wind People were still too trusting, too willing to take Forni at his word.

"Would Forni go with you?" Gan Ou asked.

"He wouldn't have much choice," Noalanon said.

The wintery quality of zir smile chilled Gan Ou, even in the bright sunlight.

It seemed that the Stone People had been pushed far enough.

"All right," Gan Ou said after a moment. "You take Forni with you. I will get the rest of the Wind People organized and heading back to Shan Yu. We'll probably fly, as that will be the quickest way there." She paused, then added, "I'm assuming that some of the Wind People will travel with you, drawing your carts for you, yes?"

Noalanon gave her a big smile. "We would appreciate that. Thank you."

"It's the least we can do, for all the help you've given us, rescuing our own," Gan Ou said.

Noalanon nodded and fell back into an easy silence.

Gan Ou joined her, staring out over the trees.

So much darkness loomed ahead of them.

Would they ever make it through? Get out of the darkness and back into the light?

GAN OU IGNORED Je Long's suggestion that she should be one of those who traveled with Noalanon and the other Stone People, back to Killapany. She'd spent most of her life there, damn it! She had no intention of returning. Ever.

Instead, Gan Ou stood with the other Wind People beside the long, four-wheeled cart. Noalanon and Forni sat on the raised seat at the front of it while Yunaki and Hirshamin sat behind them. The back of the cart was piled high with blankets, clothing, general cooking supplies for the Wind People, and the minerals that the Stone People required. Two Wind People had volunteered to travel with the Stone People back to Killapany, and had already transformed themselves into small oxen—very powerful and very quick.

They'd agreed that it was easier to use one of the carts that the Stone People had come in, though because of its size, they'd have to travel by merchant roads once they got out of the fields and plains.

The priestess of the Wind People had blessed the cart, though Gan Ou doubted that did anything other than make the Wind People feel better. Earlier, the Stone People had pulverized rocks in their hands, grinding them down to a fine powder, then sprinkled it on the wheels. The rocks had been from the pile that Hirshamin had put his name on, hopefully giving them extra power.

Gan Ou had said her goodbyes already, clasping arms with Noalanon and lying that someday, they would meet again. Gan Ou would never travel to the lands of the Stone People again, and she doubted that Noalanon would ever return to the lands of the Wind People.

Still, it was a useful, comforting fib, the kind that you'd tell children, assuring them that everything was going to be all right when the world was actually ending.

The day was gray and cloudy, with rain spitting at them. It might even snow later, despite how late the season was.

Gan Ou and the other Wind People would be long gone before then, heading north, back to their own capital, carrying news. Hopefully leaving the storm and not flying directly into it.

The Stone People waved goodbye as the cart lurched forward, the Wind People oxen as anxious as everyone else to get going.

Gan Ou stood with the remaining Wind People watching the cart disappear around the edge of the copse of trees ahead of them. The group would have to make a lot of detours around trees and lakes until they reached one of the more traveled merchant roads.

Je Long called the attention of those remaining to himself. "We must now be off," he announced importantly.

Gan Ou kept her snort to herself. As if they didn't already know that!

The group broke up into individuals, each taking care of their own tasks before helping the others. They piled the tents and cooking supplies up at the edge of the trees. One of the Wind People volunteered to act as a messenger, flying to the nearest village to tell them of the cache before heading back to her own village.

Just as they were finishing, a loud honking noise drew their attention. It was one of the scouts. They dropped out of the sky into the middle of the clearing, falling like a stone. The Wind People rushed up and gathered around them.

The scout transformed quickly out of the shape of one of the large, black-headed geese and into her Wind Person form. Her eyes were huge against her dark skin, her hair a riot of curls, adding to her wild appearance. She gratefully tore into the chunk of dried meat that someone shoved into her hands, as well as gulped some water down.

Finally, she shook her head and announced in a clear voice, "I have news."

Gan Ou rolled her eyes at the pause the messenger took. Did she really need all this drama?

"The wall is gone."

GAN OU AGREED with the others in the camp that they needed to go and see it for themselves. The wall had been haunting them, stalking them, for over a month.

Evidently, it had just disappeared, faded with the

morning sunlight. As far as the scouts could tell, it no longer existed either to the north or south of their current location.

What had happened? And why? That was the most important question.

Obviously, it had been the Bone People who'd generated it in the first place. Did they feel as if they no longer needed it? Had all of the invading force crossed over into the lands of the Wind People? Or had something happened to the Bone People who'd been creating the wall?

It couldn't be because Gan Ou and the others had rescued the last of the prisoners. That had happened a few days before. Although maybe it took a few days for the news to travel…

As one, the group of two dozen Wind People transformed into the black-headed geese and flew off to the east, toward the direction of the wall.

The primary difference that Gan Ou noticed as she flew closer and closer to the gray clouds was that it was so much clearer than it had been.

The smell of smoke was finally blowing away.

It was obvious to Gan Ou when they crossed the line where the wall had stood most recently. She felt it in her bones, a residue of magic that caressed her.

Of course, Je Long, who was at the head of the wide V of birds, didn't stop. Arrogant prick.

Gan Ou left the line and headed toward the ground.

A few followed her. She'd bet that they were the other rescuers, those who'd traveled through the wall more than once. They'd also developed an affinity toward it. Je Long was one of those who'd only made a couple of raids, as he'd stayed mostly in the camp.

Gan Ou squawked loudly as soon as her webbed feet touched the ground. The magic still inherent in the spot quickly rose up, wrapping around her ankles.

She transformed, feeling cool fog caress her bare legs. It strengthened her soul, totally unlike the times when she'd felt as though the wall was draining her.

The magic that remained was uncorrupted by the Bone People. It was the only way she could explain it.

After a moment, Gan Ou closed her eyes and *pulled* at the feeling, trying to tug that magic deep inside of her, to fill those empty spots she knew were there.

It wasn't the same as someone teaching her how to use the magic. That lack remained. Just standing there did make her magic stronger, though.

"What are you doing?" Je Long's nasal voice broke through Gan Ou's concentration.

"If you had the sense of a goose, you'd be standing here too," Gan Ou growled at him. "Can't you feel it?"

"Feel what?" Je Long asked.

Gan Ou sighed out loud and opened her eyes. "Feel the residue of the magic. This is where the wall was."

Je Long looked suspiciously at Gan Ou, his eyes narrowed. "What, so now you fancy yourself some great magician?"

Gan Ou rolled her eyes. "I can't help it if you have the sensitivity of a slug. But let the rest of us get stronger, so that we're better able to face the enemy."

Je Long pressed his lips together and glared at Gan Ou, but at least he didn't say anything else.

Gan Ou closed her eyes again and reached for the quickly fading cool stream of magic. It astonished her to realize just how much power had been poured into maintaining the wall. She felt it in her bones, the coordinated effort it must have taken. Whole villages of people, working together as one.

The Wind People would never manage such a feat. They

didn't work that way. They were much more individualistic than any of the other People.

Still, Gan Ou soaked up as much of the residue as she could. It lined those empty places she'd discovered deep in her soul, the spots where the magic should go.

When she opened her eyes, she immediately turned and looked toward the trees.

She was going to have to think long, hard, and deeply about the leaves and the wind. There was something there, somehow that she could use them…

The squawking of the herd of geese interrupted her. Gan Ou shook herself and transformed, the form coming more easily than ever.

Yes, it had been good for her and the others to stop. To refuel themselves for the coming days.

Whatever darkness was on the horizon.

GAN OU ESTIMATED that it would take the group three to four days to travel all the way back to Shan Yu. It wasn't that they'd traveled that far to the south—if she were flying by herself, she might make it in merely two days.

However, some of the group were still weakened from their captivity. They needed to rest more often than the others. In addition, Je Long insisted on stopping by some of the villages with the news of the wall, and to see what the invaders had been up to.

Gan Ou had argued that it was more important to let the elders know that the wall had been dismantled, but of course, Je Long wouldn't listen to her.

The first village they stopped at had been spared by the Bone People. They'd seen the carts draw past, but no one had stopped. The dead elk had frightened the villagers. No one could explain it.

Gan Ou couldn't shiver in her goose form, but she felt the need to when they crossed above the next village. The smell of smoke lingered in the air, not the clean smell of cooking fires but a more cloying odor that coated the back of Gan Ou's throat.

The group dropped down into the small clearing that made up the village square. Wind People were in the yards and going about their business in the small huts that surrounded the open area.

However, no one came up to greet the travelers, to offer them hospitality.

Gan Ou coughed, trying to clear her throat from the awful smell, though the air around them was clear and didn't hold any haze.

Je Long looked more angry than scared. He marched over to the closest Wind Person who was tending to a roasting fire, turning a rabbit on a spit.

"Hello!" Je Long said when the Wind Person didn't even bother to look up.

Je Long reached out and shook the shoulder of the young person.

She slowly looked up. Gan Ou could see how glazed over the young Wind Person's eyes were. It was as if she were seeing through a fog. She blinked a few times then shook her head. "What…what are you doing here? Who are you?" She stood up slowly then backed away, obviously terrified.

Gan Ou had never seen such a reaction before. The Wind People prided themselves on their hospitality. The stranger was always welcomed, not looked upon with fear.

She pushed herself forward before Je Long made even more of a mess of the situation. "We're travelers," she said gently.

The girl blinked again. Her eyes appeared to clear a little. "Travelers?" she asked. "Not foreigners? Strangers?"

"Yes, travelers," Gan Ou said, nodding encouragingly at the person.

"We like travelers," the young person said, her voice growing stronger. She gave a little gasp. "Where are my manners? I should get you food and drink. Come."

With a determined stride, the young person set off for one of the huts. Je Long and Gan Ou followed her, while the rest stayed where they were in the village square.

Walking through the village was the stuff of nightmares. The Wind People they passed all seemed to be sleepwalking. The few who weren't stared suspiciously at Gan Ou and Je Long.

"We have to kill whatever fire is creating this smoke," Gan Ou said quietly. She hadn't recognized it right away, but now she remembered how the magic of the wall had tasted like burnt sugar, coating the back of her throat.

Je Long nodded. "Send out the scouts," he said.

Gan Ou bit her tongue. While she doubted the young person would be thrilled to be serving Je Long anything at all, stopping the smoke was the more important task, though she doubted Je Long thought about it that way.

Gan Ou walked back to the Wind People who stood in the village square. They were starting to get angry at being ignored, as well as the poor hospitality that was being shown to them.

"There's foul magic operating here," Gan Ou told them. "Sniff the air."

Most of the Wind People raised their heads up to catch a better scent.

"How many feel that smoke at the back of their throat?" she asked.

At least half of the group raised their hands. Interestingly, it was most of the people who'd been raiders and had gone through the mist wall many times. They'd also been the ones who'd landed beside her and soaked up as much magic as they could.

"There's something generating this smoke," Gan Ou said. "Something magical. We need to find the source, or sources, and stop it. Be sure to tell the village folk that you're travelers in need of aid, not strangers."

"What if we find Bone People?" Ky Lee, one of the younger people asked. Her dark brown eyes looked huge in her pale face.

"Then we must stop them," Gan Ou said firmly. "Whatever it takes."

Individuals looked at each other, afraid and uncertain, though they knew what it was that Gan Ou was asking of them.

Then as one, they turned to face her again and nodded. While some of them still looked scared, the majority of them now looked determined, their expressions grim.

Whatever it takes.

***

GAN OU PAIRED the others off, trying to keep one of those who recognized the smell of the magic with one who didn't, hoping that they could learn from each other. She kept Ky Lee with herself, as the girl seemed overly scared. The teams went in different directions, searching for the source, or sources, of the bad air.

It didn't take long for Gan Ou and Ky Lee to find the fire spewing the foul smoke on the outskirts of the village, to the west. One of the Bone People attended the fire while the Wind People continued to use it for cooking, coating their meat in that awful smoke.

As Gan Ou and Ky Lee walked forward, the Bone Person spotted them. "Strangers!" she shouted, pointed at naked Wind People.

The other Wind People using the fire stopped whatever they were doing and turned to stare at Gan Ou and Ky Lee.

"Not strangers," Gan Ou said firmly. "Travelers in need of aid. Your sisters."

"No!" the Bone Person insisted as she rose up. Gan Ou would guess that she was in her mid-thirties. Her hair was an interesting auburn color and freckles covered her face. She herself was fully covered in dull colored clothing, all beiges and browns, with a decorated wide belt around her waist. "They're strangers."

"How can you call us stranger when we are like you?" Gan Ou said, remaining friendly as she walked forward. "We have been traveling and call upon your hospitality. The hospitality that Sune Li would ask you to give."

Several of the Wind People appeared to awaken at that, shaking their heads, their expressions becoming friendlier.

"Travelers," Ky Lee said, echoing Gan Ou's words. "Can you help us? We need food and clothing."

"They lie!" the Bone Person said. She drew a handful of something out of one of the large pouches tied to her belt and flung it onto the fire. "Kill them!"

Gan Ou felt herself automatically reaching for that deep pocket of magic that she'd recently discovered inside of herself. She knew it wasn't filled up with knowledge the way that it should be.

It was still the best thing that she had. She threw what she could find outward, directing it toward the fire of the Bone Person.

A strong wind blasted the fire, scattering the logs as though someone had just kicked it. The nasty cloying scent of the Bone Person's magic cleared the air.

The Bone Person looked at Gan Ou in horror, starting to back away.

Gan Ou transformed immediately into a large gray wolf. She stalked forward, snapping and growling at the Bone Person.

"You're all savages," the Bone Person said, sounding more angry than scared. "You'll soon learn the futility of resisting us." She pulled out a long knife from her belt.

For a moment, Gan Ou thought the Bone Person was going to rush forward and attack her. Her hackles raised and she gave a deep warning growl.

But the Bone Person turned the knife on herself, holding the edge of it against the bare skin of her throat. "Burn my bones at your own risk," she called out before she sliced her own throat.

Gan Ou stopped where she was, stunned. The rest of the Wind People cried out, some falling to their knees.

Without hesitation, Gan Ou transformed back into a Wind Person. It was easier this time to find those winds deep within her, to spread out the logs of the fire that the Bone Person had been using.

Ky Lee appeared beside her with a huge bucket of water, thoroughly dousing the fire, making sure it was all the way out.

"Wet the coals, too," Gan Ou said. "Then make sure all the ashes are buried."

Ky Lee nodded and went about her task while Gan Ou walked forward to the corpse of the Bone Person.

She looked like a dead person, though Gan Ou hadn't seen that many bodies. Her pale blue eyes held only anger, her mouth twisted into a vicious smile.

The body made Gan Ou distinctly uncomfortable, as if the Bone Person might be able to still see and hear them. Though Gan Ou didn't want to touch the corpse, she made herself grasp the cold, dead hand of the person and drag her further away from the cooking fire, until they were close to the trees that edged the village. Then she dropped the dead person's hand and wiped her own off on the ground, covering it with good, fresh dirt.

What had the Bone Person meant by "burn my bones at your own risk"? Was that one of the funeral rites of the Bone People? The Wind People tended not to have funeral pyres, though they had in the ancient past. Usually the body was returned to the earth to continue the cycle of life. If it was winter and the ground frozen, a corpse might be placed in a cold house until spring.

Gan Ou's hands were shaking when she reached out to tug at the Bone Person's belt. It was made out of stiffened cloth with pretty red, green, and gold stripes running the length of it. She didn't want to touch the body again, however, she had to figure out what were in those pouches.

Gingerly, Gan Ou untied the belt, then slid it out from under the body. There were half a dozen pouches, some big, some small. The largest one hung on the front, left side. Even before she touched it, Gan Ou smelled the foul magic.

Slowly, Gan Ou opened the pouch, holding it away from herself so that she wouldn't accidently breathe in any of the material inside. She carefully spilled a little of what turned out to be ashes onto the ground, then closed up the bag again immediately.

Gan Ou took a stick to stir the ashes, not wanting to touch them. There were hunks of something mixed in with the greasy ash, like bits of charcoal. There also appeared to be slivers of wood, each about the length of her finger, sharpened at one end and covered in a dark substance. It took Gan Ou only a moment to recognize that as blood.

What little food left in Gan Ou's stomach abruptly

exited, Gan Ou shaking and retching. She spat, trying to clear her mouth of the foul taste.

With trembling hands, Gan Ou carefully piled dirt on both the ashes that she'd spilled, as well as her own vomit. Then she gathered rocks and built a tiny cairn on top of each, warning people away.

Finally, Gan Ou turned back to look at the people behind her.

Ky Lee was tending to the fire, as were several of the other Wind People, bringing bucket after bucket of water to thoroughly soak the coals. They seemed angry at the fire, and were stomping on it, kicking the logs apart. One of the older men actually came up and urinated on the fire, desecrating it as a statement.

Gan Ou hoped that the same scene was being played out in the other parts of the village where such fires had been burning. Not that she necessarily wished all the Bone People dead.

At least, not yet.

THE PARTY BROKE up after the village had been cleaned. A couple stayed behind, while others went off to travel to the villages that were closest, to help the other Wind People overcome the Bone People's magic.

Je Long, Gan Ou, and one other decided to take off and fly directly to Shan Yu. They wouldn't beat the Bone People there—they'd had too great of a head start. But there had been messengers, letting the elders know that the invasion was coming. Maybe the elders at the capital had prepared themselves for the invaders somehow.

This time, there was no stopping, no breaks until nightfall. Gan Ou had to appreciate how well Je Long could fly. He was younger than she was, but she was much more stubborn.

The next morning, they rose with the dawn and took off again. The smell of smoke greeted them as they passed over the nearby villages, but they couldn't stop.

The smoke changed in nature, growing thicker, more like the haze in the wall. She also saw thick clouds rising up from the ground up ahead.

It took Gan Ou a while to realize what she was seeing.

Shan Yu was burning.

Chapter Eight

STONE

SUGAOSHI HATED that ze had been right. The Bone People did need to administer regular installments of their filth in order to maintain their control. So Sugaoshi gritted zir teeth and sat through *another* one of the stupid "prayer" sessions held by Heimir, as he spewed his filth and re-infected Mahletik and Kinrahsy.

The councilmembers sat together in their chamber, behind their grand desk, as if that might help. Sugaoshi couldn't wait until they finally ousted the Bone People. Ze would hire someone to scour the walls. Though ze couldn't see any taint, ze felt certain that the polished marble retained some of the slimy darkness spewed by Heimir.

The Bone People had politely proposed that one of them be allowed to sit with the council every time they held a session. At least they appeared to recognize the limits of their control—as soon as Mahletik raised an objection, they withdrew their suggestion.

Sugaoshi was afraid that it would only be a matter of time before the council would have to consider it, though.

Sugaoshi, Juhala, and Yagakilly had made some progress

in clearing out the taint of the Bone People from their constituents. Standing in clear view of the holy mountain and spiking their internal temperature appeared to burn out the control the Bone People had over most of the Stone People. However, those who had been infected once were much more susceptible to being re-infected.

Never clearing off the initial infection might mean that Mahletik and Kinrahsy were permanently afflicted, and could never be trusted again once the crisis was over.

At least Sugaoshi and the others had learned a tremendous amount about the Bone People, how they operated, how their magic worked. The archives had pointed the way for some of their research. For example, there were old myths of the Sea People that said that they could draw on the strength of their followers to perform their great magic. The Bone People appeared to have the same ability. When Heimir had preached to a large gathering of Stone People in the main city square, all of the other Bone People had started to sag, growing quite pale as Heimir had worked his magic.

This meant that singularly, a Bone Person wasn't that much of a threat. It was only in a group that they could truly be harmful. At first, Juhala had proposed that all they needed to do was to get rid of Heimir . However, then more Bone People had arrived in the city. The larger the group, the stronger their magic became.

One of the first things that Heimir had done was to dismantle the messenger system that Sugaoshi and the others had set up. Messages were still being passed along, but more slowly now, as the roads were being watched by Stone People who'd proven loyal to the Bone People. Sugaoshi never knew when a messenger might suddenly appear at zir door or knock on zir window.

Ze was certain that the news a messenger carried would always be bad.

Heimir himself appeared to communicate long distance with other Bone People using dark clouds that shot off after he'd called them, moving at unnatural speeds. Similar dark clouds would also approach him from time to time.

The Bone People had an affinity toward iron, like the Stone People had an affinity toward rock. The artist in Sugaoshi had been so disappointed. How much art could the two Peoples have created, if they could work with each other? How much could they have enriched each others' lives?

Instead, ze had to sit through filth bathing zir skin, trying to infect zir very soul, at least three times a week.

The temple that the Bone People had insisted the Stone People build was moving along. Sugaoshi had directed zir artists to make it beautiful, despite the ugliness of its purpose. The Bone People had demanded a six-sided tower rise up from the center of the complex, with an open balcony around the top of it.

As Heirmir tended to stand in the center of the group of Bone People when he performed his magic, Sugaoshi assumed that the tower would perform the same purpose, allowing the priests to send out clouds of control.

Finally, Heimir finished spewing his filth over the councilmembers. Sugaoshi allowed her internal temperature to fall to a more comfortable level. At least it always took the same amount of effort to maintain zir sense of self. It hadn't grown more difficult. It hadn't become any easier though, either.

After a few moments to reorient zirself, Kinrahsy gave zir report about the construction, how the temple complex was proceeding. Sugaoshi added to it, talking about the custom stonework that zir people were using to make the building beautiful.

Finally, the meeting was at an end and Sugaoshi could go back to zir work. Ze tried to spend the afternoons in the archives, searching for additional clues about the nature of the Bone People, despite the amount of work piling up on zir desk. No one had found a single mention of another People living to the east of the Wind People. But surely this wasn't the first time the two People had come into contact with one another.

The Bone People seemed to know much about the Wind People, with only a vague understanding of the Stone and Sea People. The Wind People also appeared to have a natural resistance to the Bone People's control as well. Fortunately, Juhala had managed to keep the other People isolated, sending them out of the city when ze could.

"I'd like a moment of your time," Heimir said, looking directly at Sugaoshi. "To discuss the artistic finishings of the building," he added.

The rest of the councilmembers filed out. Juhala glanced in zir direction, obviously worried. Sugaoshi still considered Juhala the least intelligent of all the members of the council, but ze did have zir uses.

"Yes, Heimir?" Sugaoshi said. Ze had already stepped down from behind the councilmember's desk, and so came to stand next to the Bone Person on the chamber floor.

Ze knew it was petty, but it always pleased zir that ze stood about a head taller than the priest.

The Bone People still wore that awful clothing that always looked uncomfortable. Today, Heimir wore a light gray long-sleeved shirt with a plain brown vest, over black woolen trousers. Sugaoshi couldn't imagine being so restricted all the time.

In response, ze wore the brightest shirts and jackets ze had. Today was no exception: ze wore a sleeveless white shirt with a peach-colored jacket that just reached zir waist, over a pretty teal-colored skirt.

"I know that you are not controlled," the priest said,

staring at zir with intense, pale blue eyes. His skin was white with pink hues, like a polished agate. Like the Stone People, the Bone People tended to wear their hair long and plaited, though the edges of it generally frizzed. Today, Heimir wore his hair loose, floating around his face.

"I don't know what you mean," Sugaoshi said, acting confused though inside, ze trembled.

What was the priest going to do about it? Ze started raising zir internal temperature.

Heimir continued as if Sugaoshi hadn't said anything. "I can tell how you hold yourself. You don't welcome my blessing, unlike Juhala and Mahletik."

"I look forward to your sermons," Sugaoshi assured him. "And to learning more about your god Valtyr." Obviously, the priest didn't know what he was talking about, as Juhala had successfully fought off the priest's control.

"I wonder if it's because you're more female than they are?" Heimir said.

"What?" Sugaoshi said, unable to control zir tone.

"You are a she," Heimir insisted. "While they are all he's."

Sugaoshi looked at him confused. "You do realize that none of the Stone People have a gender," ze said slowly. "I have no breasts. I look the same as the others."

"You wear the prettiest clothing," Heimir pointed out. "And today you're wearing a skirt."

"And yesterday, Juhala wore one," Sugaoshi said in response. "Also, I'm an artist. Of course I wear beautiful clothing. All of my life should be surrounded by art."

Heimir gave zir a thoughtful look.

Sugaoshi pressed zir point. "Which is why I'm working so hard to make your temple beautiful."

"It will be beautiful," he admitted grudgingly. "But why are you working with us? Not fighting us?"

Sugaoshi shook zir head at him. "Why would I fight you?"

Heimir narrowed his eyes at zir. "You aren't fully controlled," he said after another moment. "The only one in the council who isn't."

Sugaoshi managed to not smile at that. Stupid priest. He obviously didn't know his own failings.

"But maybe it doesn't matter, as you are only a female," he added.

Sugaoshi bristled at that. "I am neither female nor male," ze said heatedly. Then ze pressed zir lips together instead of making the threat that ze wanted to, something about having to bash the knowledge into his stupid head.

But Heimir only nodded. "My mistake," he said, before he turned and left.

Sugaoshi gave a great shake, starting at zir shoulders and going down to zir knees.

What had that been all about? Did Heimir finally not trust zir? Probably. At least he thought he controlled the rest of the council.

Sugaoshi knew that one of his next requests would be that the council get rid of zir. Which might or might not be a good thing. It would give zir more freedom in the city in which to operate. But it would also separate zir from those in power. The others would be instructed to no longer talk with zir.

They wouldn't send zir away, not at this point. They'd have to run elections again. Which weren't due until fall. The only time special elections were held was when a councilmember died in office. Or was found incompetent.

Did Sugaoshi want to fake zir own death, like the hero in the story "Malinesence"? Ze could maybe escape the city then…

Except that ze was committed to staying. Committed to learning all ze could about the Bone People.

Committed to discovering a long-term solution for dealing with them, that wouldn't involve an all-out war.

However, Sugaoshi worried that war could no longer be avoided, that the long-term solution for their woes was going to be casting the Bone People from their land and insisting that they never returned.

Perhaps even killing them.

***

SUGAOSHI MET with Juhala and Yagakilly in Juhala's office, as always. Ze still thought it was a cramped, ugly space. However, they'd settled into a routine.

The first thing Sugaoshi said when ze came into the room was, "We need to kill that priest."

It wasn't that ze necessarily felt that way. However, it was the surest proof that ze could think of to assure the others that ze still had control of zirself.

"Are you all right? What did he want? What did he say?" Juhala asked.

Sugaoshi rolled zir eyes at Juhala's breathless tone. Ze sounded like a teen waiting to find out if that other person in zir class really liked zir.

"He accused me of not being controlled," Sugaoshi said as ze sat down, accepting the hot cup of tea that Yagakilly handed to zir. "However, he does think that the rest of the councilmembers are fully under his sway."

"Did he try anything? To bring you more under control?" Yagakilly said.

Sugaoshi shook zir head. "No. Just made accusations that I was female. Female!" Sugaoshi had to put zir cup down as zir anger built. "That I wasn't important as a result."

"Interesting," Juhala said. "And that might be in line with the other things we've learned."

Sugaoshi took a deep breath, trying to pull zirself together and back from an uncontrollable rage.

"How so?" Yagakilly asked quietly.

"We have no gender," Juhala said, zir tone taking on a lecturing quality. "But all the other Peoples do. And it's important to some of the Peoples, like the Sea People, or at least, more important than it is to us."

"So?" Sugaoshi said. If only the stupid teacher would get to the point!

"We haven't been applying gender to our study of the Bone People," Juhala said. "For example, we only just realized that the males give order to the females. The females never order the males."

Sugaoshi opened zir mouth then snapped it shut again. That was idiotic. Did the males not consider the females important? Why would they do that? Even the Sea People realized that the males were valuable, though they were never as highly ranked as the females. Something to do with the offspring they bore.

"Which means that the Bone People are very confused by us," Yagakilly said, nodding. "They assign each of us a gender, then treat us as such, regardless of the truth."

"I am not a female," Sugaoshi said. By the gods, how stupid could the Bone People be!

"We know that," Yagakilly said soothingly. "They don't."

Sugaoshi took a deep breath, then another. "All right. How can we use this against them?"

"They trust the rest of the councilmembers, because they view us as male, correct?" Juhala said. "Maybe we could pretend to oust you, turn our backs on you."

"I'd thought about that," Sugaoshi said, nodding. "But you couldn't hold an election unless I was dead."

"Or indisposed," Yagakilly said. "Poisoned."

Sugaoshi gasped. "You don't think the Bone People would make that suggestion to one of you, do you?"

"No," Yagakilly said. "But we might suggest it. Carefully. Make them aware of our process. And that a solution might exist. Not that you'd have to fake your own death. You would just become too sick to attend to the meetings anymore."

"But what would I do?" Sugaoshi said. "I don't want to leave the city. I want to save my People." As ze said the words, ze felt the truth of them, deep in zir bones.

It was long past time for them to oust the Bone People. More than one hundred of the Bone People had arrived in the city. Ze didn't want to admit any more. Particularly not when Heimir and the other priests could work together in concert. Their power would only grow stronger as more Bone People showed up.

"You need to organize our People," Yagakilly said firmly. "If you no longer have your official council duties, but are still a member of the council, you can talk with People. Prepare them. Get them to cleanse themselves."

Sugaoshi nodded slowly. "Talk about how I need to continue my healing process, get them to help me? Walk them into the sunlight and have them match my own internal temperature?"

"That might work," Juhala said. "You could get to all the community leaders that way. Talk with them privately. We can keep the focus of the Bone People on us while you raise an army, ready for war."

"Why don't we just kill them instead?" Sugaoshi asked.

The other two looked at zir, surprised.

"Once they're gone, we can close our borders to them. Not allow any more to pass. We can save ourselves," Sugaoshi said, speaking the urgent words that kept zir awake at night.

"And what about the other Peoples?" Juhala said. "Do we

just leave them to be corrupted? Swallowed by the filth of the Bone People? You know that eventually, the others would come for us. And how would we determine which of the Sea or Wind People were trustworthy?"

Yagakilly nodded. "We need a long-term solution for the Bone People."

"Not just kill them all?" Sugaoshi asked, keeping zir tone light. "Forcing them back to their own lands? Letting them know that if they cross the border again their lives are forfeit?"

Sugaoshi made zirself take a deep breath, trying to contain the anger that threatened to spill out.

"One of the things we've learned about the Bone People is that they're greedy," Yagakilly said slowly. "They bargain churlishly. They also feel that they're better than all the others. Just shoving them behind a wall is only going to make them even more resentful. Force them to grow stronger before they spill out again."

"Wait," Sugaoshi said, holding up zir hand when an idea suddenly presented itself. "Greedy. Yes."

The myth of the Sea People came back to Sugaoshi's mind. The three ages. The age of greed, the age of the sea, and then the current age.

The connection was there, tenuous but possible.

The Bone People—had they been the greedy ones? In the first age of the Sea People? Whom the gods had destroyed?

While that might be possible, ze didn't see a connection with the second age, when the Sea People lived only in the waters. Still, there was something about that myth that seemed applicable to the current day.

"I need to go consult the archives," Sugaoshi said, abruptly standing. "Then, to arrange my own illness," ze added, forcing zirself to smile at the other two while all ze actually felt was rage.

Ze paused for a moment, studying zir two companions. Were they males, as the Wind People might consider such a thing? Ze had never contemplated it. Possibly Juhala, as ze tended to wear utilitarian outfits. However, ze also had a marvelous collection of skirts that ze regularly wore.

Whereas Yagakilly wore the most beautifully tailored shirts, made out of expensive cloth. How could that be considered male and not female?

It didn't matter, as neither male nor female were necessary to produce offspring. Still, Sugaoshi thought about it as ze walked back to zir own offices, planning on talking to the archivist about doing a thorough search among the Sea People's creation myth.

Afterward, Sugaoshi would go talk with a nutritionist, to see what minerals ze could take to fake some sort of disease or illness.

Yes, it would be better if ze no longer had zir council duties, had more time to talk with other people in the city.

Raise up an army.

And prepare them to kill all the foreigners.

SUGAOSHI HAD FOUND it ridiculously easy to fool the Bone People into thinking that ze was ill. Fainting in the council chambers did wonders for that, as well as having a nutritionist come in and declare that Sugaoshi needed rest more than anything else.

Heimir looked stupidly pleased with himself at the pronouncement. Had he considered that maybe it was his own "prayers" that had made zir ill? Probably not. He was too stupid to think about anyone except his own selfish wishes.

Sugaoshi spent the next few days in isolation, supposedly

healing zirself, while in reality, ze spent the time in a frenzy, painting. Ze had no idea when ze might have this opportunity again.

Normally, Sugaoshi did watercolors, bright and bold, of flowers and other things found in nature. The paintings were frequently impressionistic—instead of painting every bud in a field, ze used blobs of color to suggest a carpet of flowers.

However, Sugaoshi had trained at school and found zirself going back to a more realistic style, at least when representing the Bone People. Ze drew them in enough detail that the faces could be recognized, while the backgrounds they stood against were less realistic, bleak black and white and red buildings that towered above the Bone People, threatening to crush them.

Only once did Sugaoshi paint the holy mountain, though previously that had frequently been a theme of zirs. It stood in the center of the piece, the very top wreathed in morning clouds. The sun illuminating the mountain made its snow-covered peak glow. Using zir tiniest brushes, Sugaoshi painted people at the foot of the mountain: Stone People, Sea People, Wind People, and Bone People. Just impressions of them, though they all appeared to be in a frenzy. Ze didn't know what they were doing there. Were they worshipping? Dancing? Or fighting?

Finally, Sugaoshi felt prepared to go out and face the world again in zir new role—a recovered, though still vaguely frail entity, here to preach the word to all the other Stone People about how to keep themselves fit and well.

As well as a revolutionary.

SUGAOSHI HAD ALWAYS CONSIDERED that zir art was painting. However, ze found a tremendous satisfaction in playing a role. The Bone People of course believed zir. They were too stupid not to. It was zir own people who needed the most convincing.

Acting as a frail artist wasn't that difficult. Ze had plenty of role models, particularly among the few Sea People who ze'd met over the years. Ze did take a few more friends into zir confidence, in particular, Blythenik, the head of the archives.

Blylthenik continued the search through the ancient books and scrolls, looking for more answers. In the oldest records, ze came upon more than one reference to the Wind People actually being able to call up great winds that they then used for defense.

None of the Wind People Sugaoshi knew could do such a feat. It appeared to be yet another ability that had been lost.

How had such things been forgotten?

What delighted Sugaoshi was how ze could finally approach some of the corrupted community leaders and get them to cleanse themselves of the control of the Bone People. If ze had to estimate, at least half of the city's population had successfully been tainted. Ze worked diligently to bring that number down.

The last thing ze needed was to start a civil war among zir own people. No, they needed to be prepared to attack the Bone People. Not just force them out of the city, but be prepared to do them harm.

Sugaoshi was no longer allowed near the temple of the Bone People. Heimir still believed zir to be uncontrolled. Juhala let slip that the priest had actually suggested that Sugaoshi be completely isolated, possibly killed, so that ze couldn't infect anyone else.

Fortunately, that went against the general principles of the Stone People—no one was left alone when ze was ill. So Heimir's suggestion was easily overruled.

At least, for now.

Messengers were all directed to find Sugaoshi now. It filled zir heart with dismay to learn that the Bone People had shown up in the Sea People's lands. However, the Sea People appeared to only be susceptible to the Bone People while they were in their land form. Once they were in the water, the Bone People could no longer compromise them.

Sugaoshi relayed the information both to the other councilmembers, as well as to Blythenik one afternoon. They sat together in the cellar that held the archives. Sugaoshi had at least grown used to the smell of the old books, though ze had never come to relish the odor, unlike Blythenik and the others who worked down here.

Books, papers, and scrolls covered the main archivist's desk, along with at least three cups of forgotten tea. Sugaoshi politely ignored the stains that marred the cushions of the chair that Blythenik sat on—spilled tea, ink, and other substances best left unknown. Behind Blythenik were stacks of shelves carved out of rock and covered with books, scrolls, important letters and such.

Sugaoshi had never figured out the order Blythenik had given to all the items in zir care. If there was any order. It appeared that each archivist had come up with zir own system and started to reorganize everything, only to leave the position before ze had finished.

"Oh!" Blythenik said when Sugaoshi finished relaying zir news.

Blythenik sat still behind zir desk for a few moments, staring out into space. Sugaoshi always wanted to suggest a better tailor to the archivist. Blythenik's shirts were just a shade too loose, as if originally made for someone bigger. The archivist had skin as light as the old parchment ze cherished, pockmarked with black divots. Sugaoshi thought more than once about painting Blythenik's face, turning those marks into words or letters. Blythenik kept zir raven-black hair trimmed short, highlighting the way zir nose jutted out from the rest of zir face, emphasizing zir thin lips.

"You once related the three ages of the Sea People's creation myth to the Bone People. How they were the greedy one who the gods destroyed," Blythenik said after blinking zir bright green eyes a few times, coming back to the present.

"Yes," Sugaoshi said, nodding. The connection wasn't solid, and the Sea People, of course, wouldn't believe it. But what if the Bone People were connected somehow with their ancient past?

"And in the second age, the Sea People were only a water species. They never took their land form," Blythenik continued.

Sugaoshi merely nodded, knowing that as much as ze might want to tell Blythenik to get to the point, the archivist would take zir own precious time about it.

"So were the Sea People who only stayed in their sea form and the greedy Bone People actually part of the same age?" Blythenik suggested. "The natural defense of the Sea People is to be under the water."

"Oh, that's interesting," Sugaoshi admitted. There was no proof, would never be any proof. However, ze felt in zir very soul that the connection was there.

"Liseth is emptying out Shiboleth," Blythenik said. "The Sea People are all returning to their water form."

"And they'll die there, if they remain in the waters forever," Sugaoshi said firmly. "That's what the legend tells us."

"True," Blythenik said, nodding zir head wisely. "But what would you have them do? It's their primary defense against the Bone People."

Sugaoshi nodded, unwilling to speak the words out loud, at least to Blythenik.

The Sea People, like the other peoples, were going to have to kill the Bone People. A massive war would have to take place.

But the Sea People were even more adverse to confrontation than anyone else. They would rather just slip away.

Whereas Sugaoshi had already started arming troops. They didn't need much. Some basic training in fighting, provided by the Wind People. Practice in hardening their skin, so that they could do it on command. As well as defenses against the Bone People's mind control, such as spiking their internal temperature or turning aside.

All that Sugaoshi needed now was a clear signal from the councilmembers that it was finally time to rise up and throw off those who would try to control them.

They had a tentative plan—for the army to rise up the next time the Bone People gathered all the Stone People together for a "prayer" session. The temple complex would be complete, as would be the stone tower. However, Sugaoshi had already recruited enough stone masons that the walls and that tower wouldn't be a hindrance to them.

What the Bone People didn't appear to appreciate was that while the Stone People could put together rocks and masonry in a spectacular fashion, they could also take it down just as easily.

"Have you found anything else for me?" Sugaoshi asked Blythenik. They'd finished discussing the possibilities the Sea People's creation myth held for explaining the current day's situation.

"Only this," Blythenik said. Ze leaned across zir desk, as if to share a secret.

Sugaoshi nearly rolled zir eyes. It was just the pair of them down there. Who else was going to hear?

"Kiproary needed Sune Li's help for the Stone People to

move," Blythenik said. "They were too static on their own. And to keep the Stone People humble, ze invited Ishkra as well."

Sugaoshi nodded, though ze didn't need a lesson about their own damned myths.

"I think…I think that our myths might be a reminder as well, of the face of the abyss, the darkness that the Bone People worship," Blythenik said, pausing, "that we also need the other Peoples. None of us will defeat the Bone People on our own."

Sugaoshi shrugged. At this point, ze didn't really care that much about the other Peoples. Ze needed to rid zir own land of this disease. Forever.

"Do keep it in mind," Blythenik said, narrowing zir eyes at Sugaoshi. "It's important."

"I will," Sugaoshi said. The archivist had been right many times before. It was worth remembering, as much as ze might resent it.

Sugaoshi gladly climbed the stairs out of the dark archives, back up into the fresh air, taking deep gulps of the chilling mountain breezes.

It wasn't until ze had taken a few steps away from the stairs that ze realized that someone was waiting for zir.

A crowd of people, actually. With Heimir standing in the center of them.

"Sugaoshi, you will come with us," Heimir stated.

Sugaoshi glanced around, realizing that ze was surrounded by Stone People who, as far as ze knew, were all corrupted.

"Where are you taking me?" Sugaoshi asked, unwilling to move just yet. There was no possible way for zir to escape. None of the Stone People could run or move that quickly.

Damn it! Ze should have been more careful, should have

realized that the others would be watching zir, even as the Bone People appeared to ignore zir.

"To the temple, of course!" Heimir said. "So that we might look after you, and perhaps cure you of your malady."

Sugaoshi cursed silently. Ze hadn't thought Heimir would be clever enough to come up with a way of dealing with zir "illness" that would be acceptable to the council.

Then again, there was nothing at the temple that could hold zir. The walls were mere rock. Ze could easily escape later.

"Fine," Sugaoshi said, nodding with as much dignity as ze could muster. "I choose to accompany you. For now."

It wasn't until much later, after they'd encased zir wrists and ankles in cold metal that Sugaoshi began to regret zir choices.

Chapter Nine

SEA

LISETH WELCOMED THE CONTINUING RAIN. It had taken two days of constant downpour for all the Sea People in the city to be washed clean of the Bone People's influence.

Gunnar, the priest, as well as the rest of the Bone People, weren't quite sure what to do at that point. Liseth had imprisoned them in the former residence of the Wind and Stone People, not allowing them to further spread their filth or control.

But what should Liseth and the Sea People do now? They had stopped the first group of Bone People from doing too much damage. No one had begun construction on the temple that the Bone People had wanted them to build.

What about the next group? And the next? How could the Sea People stop the Bone People from trying to take over not just their lands, but all the lands?

Liseth needed answers. The original hunters who'd been corrupted had requested the duty of keeping watch on the Bone People. Liseth had allowed it. Not because the hunters wouldn't be influenced again by the priest, but because they were the most angry about it. They would be more diligent than anyone else as a result.

A moat had been dug around the building that held the Bone People. Any of the Sea People who entered or left the building would have to walk through three feet of water, which would bring them back to their senses if they'd been compromised. At the tolling of the prayer bells, the guards themselves would go and wet their feet. Basins of water were now kept in every room. It became second nature to wash ones' hands whenever they entered or left.

At first, the Bone People had been allowed access to the outdoors. Gunnar in particular would request to be taken to the porch up at the top of the building. The Wind People had used it frequently, flying places instead of walking out the door.

However, the third time he'd been allowed up there, he'd performed some sort of magic. First, he'd drawn dark clouds to him, then he'd cast them out. It had only taken a few moments. The priest had been well prepared.

Liseth didn't know for certain, but she wondered if that was how the Bone People communicated with each other.

She had to assume that the next group of Bone People (and there would be more groups) would already understand that the Sea People needed merely a drop of water to void the control placed on them.

Though Gunnar complained bitterly about being trapped in windowless rooms, Liseth saw no reason to let him outside again.

At least, not until they'd decided what they were going to do with the Bone People.

The regents had proposed killing them all, putting some sort of disease in their water. The vote had been close, but in the end, Liseth's vote had vetoed the action. At least for now.

They needed answers. They could always kill the Bone People later.

Liseth went to go visit her guests as the rain continued to pour from the sky. It had been over a month since they'd arrived. Fortunately, spring had arrived, with its rains. The Sea People wouldn't really be vulnerable until midsummer, when they might go a month or more without rain.

Would the Bone People wait? Time their invasion for then?

The Bone People were kept separated from each other. Liseth remembered the old myths too well, particularly since Ajooless had sent her a message via a fish. So Gunnar and the rest weren't allowed to speak or see each other, in case they could work together, use each other's strength, as the warrior Jukaless had taken the strength of her followers to do her great deeds.

Gunnar was kept in an interior room, one that had probably been used by the Stone People, as they actually didn't like the huge windows and doors that the Wind People insisted on. Bright globes of light hung from the corners as well as the ceiling, banishing the darkness. Liseth had insisted that the globes only be dimmed at night—Gunnar was never allowed access to complete night. The walls themselves were covered in white-painted brick, while the floor was dark wood.

A bed had been added to the room, set in the corner opposite the door, piled high with blankets, pillows, and furs, some of which had come from the carts of the Bone People. A dresser had also been carried into the room, made of wood with designs of leaves and vines carved around the edges of it —probably from a Wind Person's room.

Several large, sturdy chairs filled up the rest of the space, where a dozen people could have easily gathered. A hearth filled with heated stones sat against the far wall. It appeared that the Bone People felt the cold like the Wind People. As Liseth couldn't trust them with fires, she'd had Stone People volunteer to heat stones for the Bone People regularly.

Gunnar himself sat in a chair close to the hearth. He rose from his contemplation to greet Liseth when she came in the room.

A pretty green-glass bowl holding water had been placed on a stand to the right of the doorway. Liseth immediately dunked her hands in it as soon as she stepped into the room, wiping them off with a towel hanging beside it.

"There's no need to do that," Gunnar grumbled.

He wore clothing that the Bone People had brought with them, today, a gray long-sleeved shirt under a brown leather vest that still had fur attached to the inside, as well as black woolen pants and leather boots. The Sea People had removed all the pouches hanging from his belt, suspecting that they might hold magical ingredients, but they'd returned his belt to him. It was probably the most beautiful thing he wore, as wide as Liseth's hand, made out of brown leather with a rolling pattern of waves embossed on it.

He had pulled his blond hair back from his face into a tight braid that morning. His skin was a pale white with pink overtones, grown paler without any sunlight. He had green eyes that always squinted at Liseth, as if trying to find her weaknesses. His lips were thin and pink, and his smile was frequently cruel.

"Washing my hands both before and after I leave a guest is customary," Liseth assured Gunnar, though it really wasn't.

Not until now.

Gunnar sighed expressively. "But I won't try to influence your thoughts," he said.

Liseth nearly rolled her eyes. "Unlike the previous times?" she asked archly. The first time she'd visited, the priest had immediately started spewing his darkness at her. Fortunately, the guards just outside hadn't been influenced, and had made her wash her hands before she'd left the room.

Now, it was just habit.

Gunnar smiled at Liseth, trying to look earnest. "This time will be different," he said. "Promise."

"We'll see," Liseth said dryly. She wasn't about to take the priest at his word, though after the first few times, he had stopped trying, as he'd always failed.

"So what can I do for you today?" Gunnar asked. He always acted as if this were a room in his own temple and that Liseth had come to call on him for a favor.

"Answer some of my questions?" Liseth asked. "Maybe with the truth?"

Gunnar grinned at her. "Can always try."

Liseth sat down in one of the smaller chairs so that she didn't tower above the priest. He appeared to appreciate that and sat down in a nearby chair.

"What are your plans for the Sea People?" Liseth asked, starting as always with the big questions.

Gunnar shrugged. "To take over all the lands," he said soberly.

Liseth blinked. She caught herself before she made a clicking sound of surprise. "Why?" she said. This was the first time the priest had admitted to anything like that, despite how Liseth was certain that had been the Bone People's plan from the start.

"What I've told you before was the truth. Our lands are no longer as productive as they have been. There's been famine."

Liseth believed the priest. The bleakness of his tone wasn't something that could be easily faked. Gunnar had seen starvation among the Bone People.

"But why try to take over all the world?" Liseth asked. "You could have just asked for help."

Gunnar gave a bark of a laugh. "As if you would help us."

"Why wouldn't we?" Liseth said, confused.

"We are a proud People," Gunnar said after a moment, obviously trying a different tact. "In addition, we've always been taught to beware the stranger and your foreign gods. To not be corrupted by such as yourself, but to remain true to Valtyr and the abyss. You people—and your gods—turned your backs on us. Why should we seek your aid?"

Liseth sighed. What Gunnar said actually made sense. The Bone People had a very long history of not trusting the other Peoples.

"What do you know of the Wind People?" Liseth asked. She assumed that Gunnar might know the most about them, as their lands were the closest. "What myths do you have of them?"

Liseth had made sure that the Bone People understood the myths of the Sea People, so that they might know how opposed the Sea People would be to war.

"They are part animal, at least according to our beliefs," Gunnar said. He kept his tone even. Liseth believed that he wasn't being disrespectful—he was just repeating what he'd been told. "That is why they can change as they do. They've grown more animalistic over time. Which is why they've forgotten their greatest power."

"Which is?" Liseth prompted when Gunnar didn't continue.

But the priest merely smiled at her and shook his head.

"We didn't really know much about either the Stone or Sea People," the priest continued. "We assumed that the Stone People were actually made out of piles of dirt. The Sea People were part fish." He paused, looking critically at her. "You actually resemble people more than I'd expected."

Liseth marveled at all of that. It was the most that the priest had spoken since the tables had been turned on them, more than a month before. "We have no knowledge of you or your kind," she stated. "We didn't even myths or rumors of other people living to the east of the Wind People."

"Of course," Gunnar said, shrugging. "Your kind wouldn't remember. You have your simple gods. Why complicate matters with acknowledging the first, primary mover? The darkness, the abyss, itself?"

Liseth pressed her lips together and merely sighed. She kept thinking she was getting somewhere, when Gunnar would display his true arrogance again. Despite the fact that his people were now being kept prisoners, it did nothing to shake his belief in his own superiority.

"More Bone People are coming," Liseth said. "They won't be welcomed, not as you were. There are no lands here for your People. No trade. We can't trust that you wouldn't try to take over again."

"I know," Gunnar said. "And while I'd like to live in a world where we could just all get along, I don't. That's a childish, foolish idea. There will always be victors and losers. Champions and those they defeat. Those with great power protecting those weaker, but also being supported by those beneath them."

"Could we not meet on a field of strength? Become equals in your eyes?" Liseth probed. "We have our own magic, our own powers."

"That is not how the world works," Gunnar insisted. "We might get along for a while. But eventually, either we would try to conquer you or your kind would try to conquer us." He paused, then continued. "As your population expands, you will need more land on which to grow. Admit it. Eventually, you would have started taking land away from the Stone People."

Liseth peered at him, but remained silent. She wasn't about to admit that the population of the Sea People had actually been decreasing for a very long time now. Not enough Sea People were being born. There weren't as many multiple births as usual.

While the Stone People were having more multiple births than ever before.

Would the Stone People push west eventually? Try to take over the plains and wetlands of the Sea People? No, they'd be miserable there. They'd inhabit all of the mountains that ran north and south, that divided the Sea and Stone People.

But what if that wasn't enough, some year far in the future? Would the Stone People bring their rock skills with them and build more mountains, making over the places where the Sea People lived?

It was a future too far to imagine, except for the warnings of the Bone People.

Gunnar took from her silence that she agreed with him. Which she did, to a point. "Better to be truthful and show our intent now, rather than spend decades of being false friends. It's why we tried to influence you right away, as soon as we met your People, rather than waiting and establishing ourselves more firmly in your city. Valtyr would never approve of such deception."

That surprised her. She would have thought that their god, who was of the shadows, would approve of staying there.

However, if the Bone People had too much contact with another People, they might start to consider them equals, and therefore it might go against their code to take them over.

"Why did the Bone People kill all the elk?" Liseth said. The priest had answered some of her questions. She might as well see if he'd give more.

"We needed more beasts of burden," Gunnar said.

"Wouldn't it have been easier to just breed them? Or use oxen?" Liseth said. It just didn't make any sense to her.

"Remember, we're facing famine," Gunnar said sternly. "All the food we grow needs to go toward our people. The elk require no food. The magic is so simple that even a child can control one. And each elk will last for decades, possibly a century or more."

"So the elk will eventually die," Liseth said slowly.

"It will take many centuries for all their bones to be used up," Gunnar said.

Liseth had the image of a city surrounded by piles of elk bones, just waiting to be used. She couldn't help but shiver.

"And then what? You'll just kill off another entire species?" Liseth demanded.

"That's too far in the future for us to worry about," Gunnar said sternly. "We will be dead by then. As will be our children and our grandchildren. We have no idea what our circumstances will be at that point. Maybe all the People will be dead, called back to the abyss. Maybe we'll have found another solution. It doesn't matter now."

Liseth felt as though some of Gunnar's response was rote —that he'd had this argument before. Possibly with the other priests about the wisdom of killing all the elk in the first place.

"How did you kill all the elk?" Liseth found herself asking.

The smug smile that Gunnar gave surprised her. "It is not the right time for me to share that knowledge. Yet. You will know when the time comes." He stood up. "Now, I am tired. I will talk with you again in a few days."

Liseth also stood up. "Thank you for telling me what you have," she said. "I look forward to talking with you more. Learning more about your myths and about the Bone People."

Gunnar gave her a sad smile. "It won't do any good," he said. "But it hasn't been awful talking with you today."

He bowed his head to her and turned his back.

Liseth had no idea what to say in response to that. She was aware that the Bone People thought little of females.

It was just too bad that they were going to have to keep dealing with her.

She opened the door to the room, then let the guard watch as she dunked her hands into the basin, drying them off quickly before leaving the room.

The Bone People were selfish and only concerned with themselves and their immediate family. She had suspected that already.

Who else would be so short-sighted as to think that they could take over all the lands adjacent to theirs?

That they'd killed the elk because they needed the workforce almost made sense. If you had a starving People, you didn't want to give them creatures who would compete with them for food.

The fact that Gunnar was keeping the ceremony they'd used secret bothered Liseth. In fact, she'd say that he'd just threatened her some way.

No matter. The current group of Bone People were well contained. Any new groups would be turned away at the border. The lands of the Sea People were safe.

But only for now.

LISETH'S HUNTERS turned back two additional groups of Bone People that week. It was obvious that they'd been in communication with Gunnar and his group, as the first thing they did when spotting the hunters was to try to control them, without giving greetings. Fortunately, the hunters were well prepared, and had doused themselves with water before showing themselves to the Bone People.

While wearing a soaking wet shirt wasn't the most comfortable thing in the world for the hunters, it proved to be the most effective deterrent to the Bone People's magic.

Fortunately, the Bone People turned around and left as soon as they realized that their magic had no effect.

That concerned Liseth as well. What were the Bone People plotting next? She knew that they wouldn't give up. They would keep trying to invade, to use up all the lands of the Sea People as well as the other Peoples.

While most of the Sea People had returned to the land capital, some had remained in the sister water capital, and were planning on staying there until the threat of the Bone People had passed completely.

Liseth put off visiting Bayaseth and the sea capital for as long as she could. She had too much to do, too many people to see and merchants to reassure. The messengers had stopped coming regularly from the Stone People—the Bone People had gotten control of too many of their councilmembers.

Once again, Liseth sent thanks to Ajooless and her timely warning. She'd had no further communications from the girl. She'd said that she was going to continue traveling with the Bone People she'd met. But to where? Gunnar had no idea. There were many different groups traveling through the lands of the Wind, Stone, and Sea People. He didn't know where any one particular group might be heading to.

Eventually, however, Bayaseth sent a message to Liseth inviting her to tea in the marketplace. Liseth understood that was Bayaseth's unsubtle hint that it was about damned time that her sister priestess came for a visit. Particularly since they'd agreed between the pair of them that Bayaseth should not retake her land form while the Bone People were still a threat.

She was safe under the water, and would be able to lead their people if Liseth grew unreliable or had been killed.

The rain had eased off that morning, leaving the air cold and damp. Liseth felt as though the horizon was blocked by fog, their world hemmed in on all sides—the Bone People from the east, the sea from the west. More young men were gathered on the pier than she'd recalled from previous trips. Maybe they were there seeking work, to haul those who were young or too frail to Sillboden, or maybe they were worried about the Bone People suddenly appearing and they wanted a quick escape.

It didn't matter. None of them bothered her as she passed under the beautifully carved arches, walking toward the end of the pier, the wood rough under her bare feet. Come midspring, all the piers would be touched up, painted, with garlands hung on all the arches.

Would they be there to celebrate Ishkra's birthday that year? Or would all the celebrations have to take place underwater? Bayaseth had certainly hinted at such.

Yet another fight for Liseth.

She paused at the end of the pier, putting her hands together in prayer as she bowed her head. She asked for guidance as always through these dark times. However, it wasn't just for herself and the Sea People who she prayed. She also thanked Sune Li for his light in these dark times, and for the steadiness of Kiproary to support her, and even for the darkness of Valtyr to educate her and not overwhelm her.

When she was finished, she took a final deep breath of damp air and then dove into the water.

The shock of the sudden cold went through Liseth's body like a knife. She gasped, breathless, and then it was gone. The transformation came over her as quickly as the drop into the water had. She blinked once and both color and light filtered into the watery depths. Scales shot across all of her skin, bringing with them a cascade of welcome warmth. She spread her hands as webbing developed between her fingers, her feet elongating to become more like flippers.

Gills had developed on the sides of Liseth's throat, gills she knew that Gunnar had been expecting. She'd never bothered showing him her water form. Let him guess how much her people actually transformed. She knew that her teeth were now pointed and sharp, that the bony crest on the top of her head was more prominent, and that her eyes were now completely black.

The Bone People would call the Sea People animals, or fish, if they knew.

Liseth was happy to see that more of the outer rings of Sillboden were inhabited now, with people from the land capital either making their permanent residence there in the water, or at least staying for much longer periods of time.

The evidence of a People slowly declining was there, however. What little the Bone People saw before they'd been imprisoned hadn't been an accurate impression—many of the Sea People had deserted the city at Liseth's behest, something the Bone People now understood.

They didn't need to know Liseth's worries about the Sea People.

Liseth swam directly to the market teashop that Bayaseth had taken her to earlier. She waved at Bayaseth who was already ensconced at a table near the front, watching people swim by, on their way to and from the market. Liseth got her own globe full of a spicy, hot tea, then came to join her sister priestess.

They stayed floating side by side for a while. Liseth had to admit that she'd missed this. She hadn't taken much time for herself recently. It was restful to spend even just a portion of an hour sipping tea and people-watching.

Now that she thought about it, the last time she'd done this was at her last meeting with Sasuelana, her former acolyte. Though Liseth had warned Sasuelana about the dangers, her friend had insisted on staying in the city with her, in case she needed her.

It had choked Liseth up—realizing that Sasuelana was becoming a true friend.

Finally, the two priestesses finished their tea. "Follow me," Bayaseth said after they returned their empty globes to the counter.

"Where are we going?" Liseth asked as they left the marketplace then headed north of the city, instead of back to the temple complex.

Bayaseth waited to reply until they were in a fairly uninhabited section, when no one swam around them. The houses and buildings here looked deserted. No glass globes of light were strung along the walls. Algae had started creeping across the ground. Barnacles as well. The water tasted of decay, not of the fresh sea. Schools of fish darted in front of them, flashing momentarily in the light that Bayaseth cast before disappearing.

"Sometime before, you and I talked of finding the home waters of the Bone People," Bayaseth said quietly.

Liseth nodded. Though it seemed unfair to send a plague to a People who were already suffering a famine, it might be the only way to stop the Bone People from trying to take over all the lands.

"We've never found it," Liseth admitted. "Ajooless said she did—"

"But no one was able to follow along," Bayaseth said. "No one else has found it."

Liseth had to nod in agreement. Had the girl actually

found the Bone People's home waters? She did appear to have some special abilities. Or had that just been youthful exuberance?

"We have, however, been able to trace the Bone People back across the plains, to the start of the Wind People's lands," Bayaseth said smugly. "It would be possible to stop them there."

"Can we guarantee that only the Bone People would be hurt? And not the Wind People or any other?" Liseth asked.

Bayaseth merely shrugged. "You know how these things are," she said.

Liseth sighed. She did. While there was a good chance that whatever plague they developed would only affect the Bone People, there was also a chance that it would make the Wind People sick as well.

"It's a risk that we need to take," Bayaseth said earnestly.

Liseth shook her head and said, "No." It wasn't that dire. Not yet.

Even if she did believe deep in her heart that it might become that awful sooner rather than later.

"You're wrong. We need to take that risk," Bayaseth said. "Now, before more Bone People come to our lands."

"I don't want my legacy to be the destruction of an entire People," Liseth said.

"What about being the savior of the Sea People?" Bayaseth countered. "Have you thought about that?"

"You said once that I was already selfish enough," Liseth said, trying to keep her tone light and teasing.

Bayaseth merely shrugged.

The pair of them swam through a dirty current. Liseth suddenly found herself coughing. "What was that?" she asked, turning to peer behind her.

"Nothing," Bayaseth said, taking Liseth's hand and turning the pair of them forward. "Come on."

"Where are we going?" Liseth asked again. The area they'd entered was no longer merely deserted but actively decaying. Walls of what had been happy houses now lay crumbled on either side of them, the roofs long since rotted off, windows sagging, the glass broken and dirty. The water smelled foul, like sewage had been dumped nearby. No fish swam in the area. Even the seaweed that had started growing between the stones had died off.

Off in the distance, a dark cloud appeared to bloom in the water. Liseth could already feel the currents cooling off as they drew closer to that blackness.

"No. Stop," Liseth said, forcing Bayaseth to come to a halt before bringing them near. "Where are you taking me?"

Bayaseth appeared to notice their surroundings for the first time. "To see Brodalesh, the plague bringer," she said slowly.

Liseth looked forward again, at that dark spot that Bayaseth had been determinedly swimming toward. "There?" she asked, pointing.

Bayaseth clicked in surprise. "She lives just past there," she said, doubt creeping into her tone as the implications of what was before them started to sink in.

"Lived," Liseth corrected. Nothing would survive in that dark

The dark miasma loomed closer. Liseth smelled death in the water.

"What have you done?"

Chapter Ten

____

WIND

KA LEM FOUND himself dozing through the afternoons as they crossed the great plains. Though it was barely spring, the sun already beat down hard, turning the ends of the newly grown grass brown. The path the elk made through the open meadows left wisps of smoke in their wake. Flies, gnats, and other annoying insects swarmed around him. If he could bathe himself properly, he might have a chance. But the biting insects continued to hound him whenever they drove through them.

The plains were nearly featureless—just flat grasslands undulating gently in all directions. No trees or hills to break the monotony. At least the Bone People had a good sense of water, or else they knew this trail, as they seemed to drive directly from one source of water to the next.

Or maybe they were being directed. Sometimes, a dark cloud would appear, highlighted against the bright sunlight. The entire group would stop and Diethelm, the priest, would get off the cart he traveled on and stand apart from the rest of them. The dark clouds would swoop down and swirl around him for a while, before taking off to go somewhere else.

Pretty handy way to get messages from one group to the next. However, when Ka Lem asked Anjr his driver about it, she pressed her lips together and shook her head. He could tell she was scared to talk about the priest, so he didn't press.

When he could, Ka Lem worked on bringing up the winds. Though there was no one who could hear the words he spoke, he still sent them back, behind him. He figured it was as effective as a trail of breadcrumbs through the forest, where most of the small animals and birds would eat everything he dropped.

It was still better than nothing.

Sometimes Ka Lem dreamed of a whirlwind of leaves, as tall as one of the Stone People's three-story buildings, though maybe only five feet across. The leaves swirled around, teasing him. He didn't understand the significance of it. He'd never heard any stories about leaves being important to a hero.

Daleki still lived, traveling with them on a nearby cart. Cruel chains and an iron bar between zir ankles and wrists held zir immobile. Sutja, the iron worker, had figured out a combination of iron shavings and other minerals that needed to be mixed into the dirt that would get Daleki to eat.

Mere dirt held in front of the Stone Person's mouth couldn't be shoved in. Once they started mixing it with other things, Daleki couldn't hold zir mouth closed anymore. It seemed to be a survival instinct that ze couldn't overcome. Ze would eat when it was the right mineral was presented.

Ka Lem could tell that Daleki wasn't thriving, despite eating more or less regularly. Zir gray stone skin was now pocked, and white cracks had formed along zir arms.

The Bone People appeared to want to keep both Ka Lem

and Daleki alive. Why? What would happen to them once they reached the capital of Melefels?

Anjr didn't know.

They'd stopped for the night. Ka Lem had lost count of the number of days they'd been on the road. It had been two weeks, maybe more. At least the Bone People had given him some clothing so he could stay warm at night, as well as yet another blanket. His muscles ached all the time, and he knew that he'd lost a lot of strength. He wasn't sure he'd even be able to stand when they finally unchained him.

Anjr handed him the hunk of bread that he usually got for dinner, as well as a small bowl containing a thick stew.

Ka Lem always stopped and gave thanks to Sune Li before he ate. Diethelm the priest had stopped "praying" over him on a regular basis, so Ka Lem's thoughts were always his own. He still moved his feet in a dance whenever he could, as they traveled through the long days.

He found Anjr staring at him as he ate that night. "What is it?" he asked quietly. She'd continued to be friendly to him as they traveled, though he didn't trust her. She told him about the Bone People and he tried to teach her about his own, though frequently she would just leave rather than hear about the ones her People had kept imprisoned. She was much happier to hear about the Sea People, though still, only so much.

"Sometimes it's amazing to me that we're feeding you," Anjr said. "The priest wants you alive."

Ka Lem nodded, thinking. He'd heard mention of a famine before. "You were hungry once, weren't you?" he said, hoping to get more of the story from her.

Anjr sighed and stared off into the distance, her eyes seeing something very different than the plain stretching before them. "The crops failed one spring, when I was twelve," she said softly. "The village had already depleted the winter store. But it wasn't just our crops. It was as if an illness ate everything that grew. The fruit trees. The grasses. The berry bushes. Everything."

She shivered, a deep cold still lingering in her bones.

"Our village used to be beautiful," she said, sadness tinging her tone. "We killed most of the trees nearby, trying to eat the interior of the bark. I used to wake up to birdsong every morning. None of the birds sang that summer. Very few have come back. My hunger was like a living thing in my distended belly, always clawing to get out."

"What did you do?" Ka Lem asked, horror filling him as he put the stew to the side.

"We survived," Anjr said, her voice bitter. "At least the healthy people did. Many of the elders died, as did quite a few of the babies. The next spring, farmers had to hire guards to keep the crops safe, or else people would have stolen the grain before it could be harvested. Same with the fruits and berries."

"Are the crops coming in regularly now?" Ka Lem said, prompting her to go on.

Anjr shrugged. "Some years. But never as good as they had been. There's never enough food to go around. People starve. Every year now."

"I'm sorry," Ka Lem said. He guiltily picked up the bowl of stew again.

"The elk don't eat anything," Anjr admitted quietly.

Ka Lem blinked, then nodded. "I see," he said. Though he didn't. Not quite. "What were you using before the elk?"

"Horses," Anjr said. "They were created by the priests, like the elk."

Ka Lem swallowed down the bile that rose up. Though he'd only suspected that had been what had occurred, Anjr had just confirmed it.

"However, all died the horses with the famine. Even though they didn't eat anything either."

The Bone People had killed all the horses, taken them, and used their bones to create creatures that they could use. Creatures who didn't eat, didn't sleep, and lasted for a long while.

What would they take once the elk died?

"I'm sorry the Bone People had to go through that," Ka Lem said. None of the Wind People had ever experienced a famine. Neither had the Stone or Sea People

Anjr shrugged. "We need different land," she said earnestly, turning her bright gaze on him. "We need to be able to feed our People."

"We would have traded with you," Ka Lem said.

Anjr shook her head. "You turned your back on our god. Why would you help us?"

Ka Lem knew he could argue, but that Anjr wouldn't believe him. So he finished his stew in silence and handed her the bowl, saying, "Thank you."

He appreciated the food more than ever before, particularly since it was so precious to the Bone People.

Anjr left and Ka Lem was alone with his thoughts again. What were the Bone People planning? Why were they taking him and Daleki?

Would he ever be able to escape? Or would they skin him and use his bones for something?

━━━━━━

KA LEM PERKED up as the wide path of grass turned into a rutted dirt road. They were finally approaching the lands of the Bone People. He looked around him eagerly. Off in the distance he saw a small compound of buildings.

While the Wind People worked primarily with wood, the

Bone People worked with iron. So instead of having rounded homes with the wood smoothed over so that the planks and trunks appeared to have grown together, the Bone People's homes were built square, out of flattened boards. (Anjr explained later about metal nails used to attach the boards together.) The roofs were flat as well. Ka Lem would bet they had very little snow or rain in the area so the roofs didn't need a peak.

The group didn't pass close to the first compound that Ka Lem spotted. He guessed it was a large family farm, with several smaller buildings clustered around a long great hall. A short wooden fence ran around it, the boards running lengthwise between the posts.

Beyond the fence, Ka Lem spotted at least two goats and a couple of chickens near the long hall. He didn't see any people, or any elk.

No, wait. After they passed the compound, Ka Lem spotted the farmer and his family out in the field. Their plow was being drawn by two of the dead elk. The children followed behind, sowing seeds carefully, planting them just so, making each and every one count.

Ka Lem's People kept much smaller fields. Then again, they tended to harvest as much from the forests around their villages as the fields themselves.

The group passed a copse of tall maples and birches, before the next field started.

Ka Lem's unease grew.

Had there been more forests in this area at one time? They continued to pass small stands of trees, and the houses were all made out of wood.

Had the greed of the Bone People destroyed one of their greatest resources, the woods all around them, leaving them dependent on fields that could fail?

Later that afternoon, the group passed through a small

village. Ka Lem studied it carefully as they rode on, not stopping, swinging his head from one side to the other, trying to take it all in.

The buildings were mostly made out of wood, a single story, with slightly slanted roofs, the back a little higher than the front. Barrels sat at the corners of the houses, with spouts leading from the roofs, collecting rainwater.

So he'd been right—this was a dry area.

Metalwork decorated many of the houses. Doors were made out of wood, with pretty swirling patterns of metal running across them. Low rock walls surrounded many of the houses, and fancy iron gates made out of curved rods closed them off. There weren't many crops growing in the front yards. Ka Lem wondered if that was because of the famine or something else. He did see a few chickens. Quite a few places had elk waiting just outside the fence, staring into space.

While most of the buildings were made out of wood, a few appeared to be composed of rocks. It took Ka Lem a few moments of study to see that fine metal mesh had been strung on either side of posts, then the space between the two lengths of mesh was filled with small stones. More metal had been melted between the rocks to completely seal the walls.

Straight paths led away from the main road, as if each had carefully been laid out, instead of following natural lines or curves. The road went by what was probably the village square, again, the lines neat and the angles sharp.

Why was that? Was there a significance to that? Ka Lem had never seen such straight angles before.

He speculated that all the villages had the same shape. The Bone People he traveled with had a particular pattern that they always used when making camp.

The few villagers that the group passed looked on the

carts with curiosity, but no one from the village came out to greet them. Had they been warned away? Or was it custom?

Ka Lem thought the villagers seemed poor. They wore the same sorts of clothing that the group around him wore— long sleeved shirts, long skirts or pants, most of their skin completely covered.

However, the clothing itself looked poorly made. It was all dull colored, browns and grays, no greens or reds, or even a true black. They all wore cloth belts as well—no leather— and frequently the belts were just an inch or two wide.

That night, when the group made camp, Ka Lem asked Anjr about that. "Why do you cover up your bodies all the time?"

Anjr blinked at him in surprise. "We're not covering our skin," she said. "It's the bones." She held her hands up and looked at them. "Fine ladies even wear gloves all the time. There's a few in the court who sometimes wear masks as well." She switched her gaze back to him. "The bones matter. The skin covers the bones, protects them. It's important to give the skin extra support for protecting the bones."

That almost made sense to Ka Lem. He could see the great magic that had been done with the elk bones. "What else can you do with the bones? What magic? Besides make creatures like the elk?"

"You don't use bones, do you?" Anjr said. She nodded to herself. "The great war chief Katyr threw a bone into a pot of water and fed his troops for a week on it. The bones always know where water lies, too, in the hands of the right priest." She stepped closer, then said softly, "There's even a story of a female who used a bone to disguise herself as a male, taking on the form of her husband to avenge him."

"Interesting!" Ka Lem said. "I would love to hear more of your tales." He had trained as a teacher. The stories of the other People had always been fascinating to him.

Anjr leaned closer and dropped her voice more. "When someone dies, you have to burn their bones proper. That way, the smoke lets the family know of their death, even if it's hundreds of miles away. But you have to be careful, or the soul that rises with the smoke can be captured and enslaved."

"What else can you do with bones?" Ka Lem said, not allowing himself to react to that. It seemed that the Bone People were all comfortable with enslaving other people, a new term that he'd had to learn.

"Some say that if you plant them just right, they'll grow into a fearsome hut that no one else can enter," Anjr said. "And they can direct the clouds."

Ka Lem nodded. So somehow, the priests used bones when they directed the dark clouds they used to communicate with others.

"And what about—" Ka Lem started when another voice interrupted them.

"So I see we're educating our prisoner about our myths," Diethelm said, a false heartiness to his voice.

Anjr stiffened. Ka Lem didn't care for the fear that crossed her face, though she replied smoothly, "As you wished."

"Good, good," Diethelm said.

The priest looked tired. Ka Lem wondered if it was just the constant travel or something else. His brown eyes had faded, and dark circles marred his pale skin. Lines ran around the corners of his wide mouth. If Ka Lem watched carefully, the priest's hands sometimes trembled as well.

"We are going to be going through many villages, soon," Diethelm said. "Now, I cannot allow you to sit without the chains. However, I know that you would like to present a better appearance. At the next river, I will have you dunked and bathed."

"Thank you," Ka Lem said. He'd been itching to have a

bath, to clean his skin. He hoped that by leaving the plains that he'd be bothered less by biting insects. Getting himself really clean would help as well.

"Good, good," Diethelm said. "Have a good evening," he added, nodding to Anjr then walking away.

Anjr had grown completely pale. Her wide eyes seemed to now take up most of her face.

"What is it?" Ka Lem asked quietly. It was as if the priest had shown her all of the spirits of her ancestors, and all of them enslaved.

Anjr shook her head and raced away.

Something the priest had said had frightened her badly. Was it because he'd wanted to bathe Ka Lem in a river? Was there something significant about the river? Or the act of bathing, itself?

THE NEXT DAY, about midmorning, the group approached a large river they called Stotram. Flat-topped merchant boats with stacks of wooden crates sailed up and down the river, their sails made from brilliant blue and red material—the most colorful cloth Ka Lem had seen since passing into the lands of the Bone People.

The Stotram was wide enough that the group had to cross over it on a bridge that was broad enough for two carts to pass side by side. The piers sinking into the water appeared to be made out of huge stones, held together with long flat metal bars. Wooden planks formed the top of the bridge, held in place with what Ka Lem guessed were large iron bolts.

Ka Lem kept expecting for the group to pause before they crossed the river, but they didn't. Maybe the Stotram wasn't the river Diethelm had in mind.

Once they crossed over the river, the group split in two. Diethelm's cart, as well as Ka Lem's and Daleki's, all turned off the main road and started following a much smaller path, rutted and overgrown, heading north along the bank of the river. Ka Lem could just see Anjr's head and shoulders above the pile of goods strapped to the front of the cart on which he rode.

It wasn't his imagination that she'd grown stiff with fear.

The group turned again, heading west. They now traveled beside a much smaller stream that fed into the main one. It was less than ten five feet across. The banks were steep though, as if the water had been much deeper at one time. Reeds grew along the edges, waving in a breeze Ka Lem didn't feel.

They passed under a wide arch. It took Ka Lem a moment to realize that the skulls of people decorated the entire white-stone structure. He also recognized elk skulls, as well as what he thought might be horse skulls. Long leg bones ran up and down the pillars.

Ka Lem wasn't sure where they were, but he knew that this had been what Anjr feared.

The delicate scent of smoke wafted around them. It had a sweet tinge to it, as though cedar wood burned in the fire.

Or maybe that was the smell of burning flesh. Ka Lem's stomach churned.

The cart bounced hard over the rocks, jarring his teeth. They passed out of the open and into a copse of trees. The sudden shade sent cascades of goosebumps down Ka Lem's back. It smelled like wet moss, and the track changed from dirt to mud.

Finally, the carts came to a halt. Ka Lem looked around, identifying the trees easily: birch, maple, even a couple of different pines. Ferns grew large in the shade of the trees. The smell of smoke grew stronger. The wind carried the sound of chanting, but it wouldn't tell him what was going on behind him, what the priest was doing.

The riverbank had disappeared in this location. Instead, a small sandy beach ran down to the water. The sand had to have been carted there, as it was white and grainy, not brown like the river itself.

After what felt like a long while, Diethelm came back to Ka Lem's cart. Two guards came with him. Anjr stayed where she was, on her seat, rigidly looking forward.

The priest started chanting a prayer of thanks to Valtyr, for the abyss that formed all, influenced all, was the basis for everything. How even the brightest of days was followed by the blissful night. How the cycle passed from life into death and back around again.

The two guards didn't look at Ka Lem. They worked at releasing the chain that ran between the shackles around his ankles from the two huge loops bolted to the back of the cart. Then they picked Ka Lem up between them, as if he weighed nothing.

Maybe he did at this point—maybe he'd grown as light as the wind. Or the guards had been blessed with extra bone strength by the priest when they'd first stopped.

The guards halted at the edge of the river. Ka Lem couldn't tell for certain, but he'd bet that they were scared to go into the water. Instead, they heaved Ka Lem into the center of the river.

The cold of the water shocked Ka Lem, making him gasp and breathe in the water. He found his feet and shot up, driving his head back above the surface. It was only then that he realized the water was only about waist deep where he was. The river itself probably didn't get much deeper than that.

He sputtered, blowing water out of his mouth and wiping off his eyes. What in the world had just happened?

The guards stood on the side of the river and looked out at him. They held onto the chain that connected Ka Lem's ankles. They didn't do anything else, just stoically held onto him, while Diethelm continued his chant. He talked about the blessings of the river Jollr, and how out of one would come many.

Ka Lem wasn't sure what they expected him to do. He'd already gotten a mouthful of the water. It had tasted sweet, and he couldn't sense anything poisonous about it.

The priest had told Ka Lem that he could bathe if he wanted to. So he did. He dunked his head back under the water, scratching at his scalp, trying to get his hair clean. He scooped up a handful of sand and pebbles and scoured his skin, washing away the dirt and grime. He even took a mouthful and rinsed his mouth, blowing out the water in a long stream.

He thought about walking closer to the shore, splashing water at the terrified guards. He wasn't certain what scared them so much about the river. But something did. That archway they'd passed under had definitely been warning people away from water.

Finally, Diethelm finished his chant. The guards started tugging on Ka Lem's chain.

He debated resisting them. But he doubted that would do any good. They'd merely drag him out of the water, and his now mostly clean back would get covered in the dirt and sand of the bank.

So he walked out, the guards backing away as he did so, trying to avoid any contamination.

Diethelm himself held out a towel for Ka Lem to use to wipe himself down. It was a chamois cloth, about three foot square, bleached almost white and incredibly soft. It was the best piece of cloth that Ka Lem had seen any of the Bone

People use. He couldn't imagine why the priest had handed it to Ka Lem to use for drying himself off.

When Ka Lem finished with the cloth, Diethelm held out a basket for Ka Lem to put the cloth into. Then he shut the basket tightly, as if containing any ill effects carried by the water.

It surprised Ka Lem when the priest next handed him a long robe. It was made out of an off-white linen with long sleeves, that covered him completely down to his ankles. A matching belt tied it shut. There was no decoration on the material, no fancy stitching. He felt the quality of the cloth. It had been finely woven.

When Ka Lem put it on, he realized that it was the most dressed he'd been since he was captured.

Ka Lem suddenly realized that he was being dressed for some ritual. Something to do with bathing in the water that terrified the Bone People.

After Ka Lem had been re-secured back on his cart, the priest spent some time blessing the guards. He used a bone wand, passing it over their legs and arms.

Was that just Ka Lem's imagination, or did the guards now appear to have a slight shimmer around them? As if they'd just been shielded?

The guards disappeared for a moment, then reappeared again carrying a large half barrel between them. Now, they stepped into the river gingerly, filled the barrel, turned around and went to the other cart.

It took Ka Lem a moment to realize that the guards were still dry. Whatever spell the priest had cast, it protected the guards from the water.

They lifted up the barrel and dumped it over Daleki.

The Stone Person shuddered, but then didn't move again.

Why hadn't they given Daleki the chance to walk into

the river on zir own? Was it because even as hobbled as ze was, ze could still overpower the guards?

Then again, Ka Lem had never heard the Stone Person speak, not once, since they'd been captured. Ze did smile sadly at him when ze had the chance, but ze had never said a single word.

Whereas Ka Lem had tried to talk with Anjr all the time.

The guards dumped a second barrel on the prone Stone Person, then brought the barrel back to the priest. He waved the bone wand over the barrel once, blessing it? Removing all the moisture from it? Ka Lem wasn't sure.

But the guards now seemed satisfied and carried the barrel away.

In just a few moments, the carts started up again, traveling next to the river for a few miles before they stopped again, just for a moment.

As Ka Lem's cart drew closer, he realized that a gate had barred the exit. One of the guards now stood beside it, holding it open.

Bleached white skulls hung from the iron posts that made up the gate. A plaque containing scrolled letters warning of death ahead took up most of the center of the gate.

The river Jollr wasn't to be trifled with.

Ka Lem still wasn't sure what made it so deadly. The water in his hair dried quickly. His skin didn't break out into a rash, nor did his stomach suddenly start to churn.

Yet, Anjr didn't appear to relax again until they were far away from the water.

———

KA LEM HAD HOPED that perhaps, now that they were in

a town and he was wearing clothing, that they might actually allow him inside of a building.

That was not to be.

Instead, the guards put a tent up right over where his cart had been set, in the front yard of what looked to be a large inn. He saw dozens of Bone People walking through the yard, into and out of the building. Many stared at him with huge eyes, obviously frightened by what they saw.

He'd been marked. That much he knew. Probably for some sort of sacrifice.

It wasn't until much later that evening, long after sunset, that Anjr approached Ka Lem.

"Do you want to know how the priests made the elk?" she asked quietly.

Her face was hidden in shadows, so Ka Lem couldn't see how she looked. Her voice, however, sounded defiant.

"They brought a herd of them from your lands," she said quietly. "A dozen in all. They walked them through the towns, along the main merchant roads, before they brought them to the Jollr river."

Ka Lem found a sudden lump in his throat, stealing his words.

"They walked the elk through the river, bathed them and watered them there, before slipping wreaths of sacrifice around their necks. Off-white linen, finely made."

Ka Lem wasn't sure if Anjr could see him, but he couldn't speak, could only nod, asking for her to continue.

"The elk were taken to Melefels, where a great ceremony was performed. First came the dance of a thousand knives. Each priest would walk by and cut an elk. So many priests, so many cuts. No one could claim that he was the one who finally caused the death of the elk. Then the bones were removed from the bodies and the priests reassembled the bones, animated them with all the little deaths from the cuts."

"What are you saying?" Ka Lem finally managed to whisper.

"The priests didn't need to take a dozen elk and kill them, in order to create the elk we now have," Anjr said flatly. "They only needed one."

With that, she turned and fled into the night.

Ka Lem felt the stew he'd had for dinner that night suddenly turn in his stomach. He understood the guard's fear of the water, how touching it might mark them for death.

They only needed one.

One elk. One Stone Person. Or one Wind Person.

In order to kill, and then enslave, all the rest.

Chapter Eleven

STONE

NOALANON STOPPED the cart drawing them forward when ze felt the land change. Hirshamen nodded. Ze had felt the change as well.

They'd finally crossed the border from the Wind People's land to the Stone People's.

It all looked the same on both sides of the border. There was nothing to mark the spot. Just the feeling.

They were in the foothills, having left the forests and meadows of the Wind People two days prior. Hard gray granite lay under a covering of short grass, the comforting rock peeking through whereever the grass grew thin. Up ahead, water pooled in a shallow pond that would melt away with the summer heat. Birds of prey circled above them in lazy circles.

Noalanon slipped off the cart eagerly, zir toes reaching for the supportive land. Ze gasped as the shock of being *home* spiked through zir. Ze found zirself growing completely motionless as the land made itself known to zir.

The holy mountain as well. It stood to the north. With zir eyes closed, ze turned zir face to it unerringly, then breathed deeply, as if ze could already smell the clean breezes blowing from the mountain top.

When Noalanon opened zir eyes, ze found Hirshamen had been doing the same thing, standing there and breathing, face turned toward the mountain. Yunaki had joined them, though ze stood just watching the other Stone People.

Obviously, Yunaki had never given birth, or been a teacher. Ze didn't feel the change of the land as sharply as the other two.

Noalanon looked around trying yet again to spot the difference. They'd crossed out of the woods and into the foothills two days before. Ze had assumed that as soon as they left the flat lands of the Wind People that they'd be in the Stone People's territory.

It appeared, however, that the two People shared the foothills.

Forni stayed where he was on the cart, watching all of them curiously. Noalanon wondered if, in a different time, Forni could have been a teacher, as he appeared to have a great desire to learn more about the Stone People.

Except that sometimes…Noalanon suspected he sneered at their differences, instead of celebrating them.

No matter. Forni was a long, long way from his home, surrounded by zir kind, now.

Noalanon paused for a bit longer, reaching for that bedrock connection with Jolapen. It didn't surprise zir that ze felt nothing at the moment. Generally they only connected at night, when they were both alone and near sleep. It still disappointed zir a little—ze had wondered if perhaps they would be able to connect better once ze reached zir own lands.

Finally, the three Stone People climbed up onto the cart and they continued north along the rutted, rarely used merchant road that traveled from the south up toward the capital.

Forni asked zir as soon as they started, "So we're in the lands of the Stone People now?"

"Yes, we are," Noalanon replied. Ze tended to be the only one who answered Forni's questions. Yunaki didn't have the patience, and Hirshamin didn't like the Bone Person at all.

"How did it feel?" he said, gazing at zir intently.

Noalanon tried to put the feeling into words. "It's like—before, I was always walking uphill. Not a steep incline. But I had to fight to put one foot in front of the other. Now, the land has leveled out, or perhaps there's a slight decline now. It's easier. Plus, the land supports me here. It pillows my steps, makes everything smoother." Ze shook zir head. It was going to take zir some time to figure out the differences between the two lands.

"I felt nothing like that leaving the land of the Bone People," Forni said thoughtfully.

"Not all the Stone People feel the difference," Noalanon said. Yunaki definitely didn't have the same sense of the Stone People's land that Noalanon and Hirshamin did.

"Why is that?" Forni asked. He seemed surprised.

Noalanon merely shrugged. Ze wasn't about to tell him the theory that ze and Daleki had come up with, how those who had given birth had a stronger connection to the land than others.

That would give Forni an excuse to talk yet again about gender, and how the Stone People were really gendered if they would just allow themselves to be.

Noalanon nearly snorted to zirself. Forni insisted that Noalanon presented as female, while Hirshamin was male. This was, in part, due to how broad Hirshamin's shoulders were, as well as the fact that ze worked as a builder.

What would it do to Forni's precious theories when he

learned that Hirshamin actually had carried over half a dozen offspring?

No matter. Forni would learn in his own place and time.

"Why do you think that the Bone People don't have as good of a sense of their land as the other People?" Noalanon said, deflecting Forni's comments.

"I think our land has turned against us," Forni said seriously. Sadness tinged his words, as it frequently did. "I don't know why. But while we might claim it as ours, it doesn't claim us as its."

Noalanon thought that was an interesting interpretation —that the land claimed its People as much as they claimed it. That implied more consciousness in the very ground itself than zir people were usually willing to give.

And yet...ze felt the stones here. Felt as though ze could talk with them. Wondered about the stone container that ze had awoken—would it start speaking to zir now? Could ze use it as a guard, have it tell zir about anyone who passed nearby?

"I don't know if our land has claimed us or not," Noalanon said after a few moments. "But the holy mountain...maybe."

"What do you mean?" Forni said.

"Even in the lands of the Wind People, I always felt as if I knew where the holy mountain was," Noalanon said. "And now, I'm sure of it. There's a reason why that mountain is holy to us and to Kiproary."

Forni nodded. "I will have to see if it is holy to my god as well," he said. "I would argue that it is."

Noalanon pressed zir lips together and didn't reply. Ze didn't want to get into yet another argument about the gods, either. Forni's superiority irritated everyone, even the two Wind People, currently transformed as small oxen, who drew their carts so quickly every day.

After a few moments, Noalanon found that Forni still stared at zir. "What is it?" ze asked after a bit, though ze suspected that even if ze never asked, he would still let zir know what was on his mind, the thoughts welcome or not.

"You seem more like people, now," he admitted. "It wasn't as if you were merely a pile of rocks that could move, before," he hastened to add. "But you have more life."

Noalanon nodded. Gan Ou had mentioned that as well, that in their own territory, the Stone People seemed more alive, and that in the Wind People's territory, they were more rocklike.

"As I said, it's easier here," Noalanon said. The land supported zir.

"I can tell," Forni said. He squinted at zir for a few moments, before turning his gaze forward, settling into his own deep thoughts.

Noalanon would have to ask him at some other time about why he thought his land had rejected his own people. Then again, how often did the Bone People bless the firmament on which they walked? They worshiped the abyss, the darkness, the night, not the day and the world. They looked forward to being taken back into their god's endless blackness, to be back in his embrace, instead of trying to gain wisdom to carry into the next life.

Then ze faced forward zirself. Just a few more days—a week at most—and ze would be reunited with zir own true love.

Despite the war, despite the invasion of the Bone People, Noalanon still had something to look forward to.

NOALANON COULDN'T BELIEVE what ze was hearing from the messenger they'd run across after traveling for several days in their own territory. Evidently, the Bone People had already arrived in the Killapany and taken control of the council. Zir own people were building a temple for Valtyr. The Sea People had been contending with the Bone People as well.

"Why didn't you warn us about this?" Hirshamin demanded, turning on Forni.

For a moment, Noalanon wondered if Forni had been shocked by the news, or pleased. Now, he looked appropriately scared and took a step backwards from the fury directed at him.

"I didn't know!" he proclaimed. "How could I know? I knew that there were many groups, all self-contained, leaving our lands. How could I know where they were going? Like you, I just assumed that they'd all be going to the lands of the Wind People."

Hirshamin merely growled, then stalked off. Yunaki walked away as well, taking the messenger and the two Wind People back toward the campfire they'd set up, promising food, drink, and companionship for the evening. That left Noalanon and Forni standing alone on the edge of the firelight.

Even in the dimness, Noalanon could see better than the Bone Person, and so could see Formi's face well. Ze knew it was petty to be delighted that the Stone People could see better in the darkness than the Bone People, who worshiped the abyss. Ze couldn't help the trickle of pleasure it gave zir every time ze thought about it.

"I didn't know what was happening in Killapany," Forni said earnestly. "How could I know?"

As had happened more than once, Noalanon had the impression that the Bone Person lied. "It seems that the Bone People communicate with each other using dark clouds," ze persisted, something ze hadn't known before, that the messenger had told them.

"Only the priests can use those," Forni said.

That, Noalanon sensed, was the truth. And Forni had always claimed to be a slave.

"Are you a priest?" Noalanon asked after a moment.

Forni stared at zir. Finally, he dropped his head and looked at his feet. "I once trained with one, yes." Then he looked up, meeting zir eye directly. "But I never took the final vows. I'm not a full priest."

Noalanon would bet that Forni was telling zir the exact truth, without a single word of deviation to one side or the other of that fine line.

"Can you read the dark clouds? Gather the messages sent along with them? Use them yourself?" Noalanon pressed.

Again, Forni looked down at his feet. "Sometimes," he admitted. "But none of those messages are meant for me!" he added. "I can read them, sometimes, as they race by. None have approached the camp, though. None have been directed at me."

Was he telling the truth? It was possible.

"Tell me about the clouds used as messages, then," Noalanon said. Ze folded zir arms over zir chest, prepared to wait all night if need be.

Forni pressed his lips together tightly, obviously thinking hard.

Noalanon knew that he didn't want to tell zir a thing about them. He also realized, however, that he had to say something.

"The priests can sometimes call a piece of the abyss to themselves," Forni said slowly. "It takes great power to generate one. I can't do it by myself."

Noalanon stood silent, as stubborn as the mountain.

"Once one is created, it can carry the words of the priest.

It can also be directed toward another priest. But not just any priest. You have to direct it. Specify who it should go to."

"By name?" Noalanon said.

"Name, yes, that's best," Forni said. "Title sometimes works too, though frequently, more than one priest will have the same title, and so the messenger from the abyss merely finds the first, closest priest bearing that title."

"How fast do the messages travel?" Noalanon said.

"As fast as the wind. Faster than we're traveling," Forni said.

He wasn't in full control of his features, or he'd forgotten how well Noalanon could see in the dark, because otherwise, ze didn't think he'd sneer that way.

"How much information can a message carry?" Noalanon said, determined to learn more.

Forni shrugged. "Depends on the size of the cloud that was first created," he said. "The bigger the cloud, the longer the messages. Could be, maybe, a full speech, the largest ones, that is."

Noalanon blinked. That was a really long message that could be sent. Particularly when compared to the Wind People. A single wind of theirs could carry maybe a half dozen words at most.

"When a priest receives the message, what does he do? Does the cloud disperse?" Noalanon said.

"No," Forni said. He looked a little angry, now. He didn't want to be telling zir any more.

"So what does the priest do?" Noalanon said. "Does the priest listen to the message then send the cloud to the next person? Or maybe the next priest with the same title?"

"I don't know," Forni lied.

"Can the cloud be used to carry someone else's reply, back to the original sender?" Noalanon said, pressing on.

"Yes," Forni said grudgingly. "But the return message has

to be shorter. And if the two priests are having a conversation, the messages get shorter and shorter until all the power of the abyss is drained away. Which may happen in midflight, if the priests aren't careful."

Noalanon nodded. That made zir decision easy. "You will be watched at night from now on," ze said.

When Forni looked as though he might protest, ze went on. "The others barely tolerate you. None of us trust you. This is merely a way of protecting ourselves, though a message is never coming to you again, right?"

"No messages were ever directed to me before," he repeated. "They're not about to be directed at me now."

Noalanon believed that. However, what ze had said was true. There were too many things about the Bone People that they still didn't know, despite having traveled with one now for a few weeks. Too many things that Forni claimed to not know about, questions he wouldn't answer directly.

Still, Noalanon wasn't sure what else the Stone People would do with him. They couldn't just outright kill him. That wasn't in the nature of zir people.

Or at least, it never had been before now.

THE NEXT MORNING, Noalanon, Yunaki, and Hirshamin all practiced spiking their internal temperatures quickly. Just a small boost was undetectable. They taught themselves to grow hot enough that their skin would glow at a moment's notice, based on the information the messenger had told them. Their clothes smoked when they got that hot, but that was acceptable. They needed to be able to protect themselves, as they were traveling into a hostile situation.

Since they'd been part of the original group that went to support the Wind People, they all still had the ability to harden their skin instantly as well. They spent some time practicing that, too.

It was all they could do against the unknown.

At the next small village, they said goodbye to their two Wind People who had brought them so far, buying small oxen favored by the merchants instead.

The Wind People left soon after lunch that day, transforming into large geese who could travel more quickly than the oxen. No one knew what was happening in the lands of the Wind People, and they were anxious to get back to their homes.

The villagers hadn't seen a Bone Person before. While many of them tried to contain their curiosity, the others merely stared at Forni. He was paler than any of the Wind People, and his hair was the color of gold in the right light. He continued to wear clothing that made him comfortable, being fully covered at all times. At least he knew enough to keep his opinions to himself about sleeveless tops and short skirts.

Hirshamin talked with the few builders they had in the village, showing them how to put their names on the stones, with great success. Earlier, Hirshamin had tried to show the messenger the same trick, but the messenger hadn't had the touch.

Forni watched in amazement. It appeared that bringing the stones to life had never been an ability that he'd even considered possible. He nodded at Noalanon and said, "Your land has truly chosen you."

"Why do you think your land has turned away from you?" Noalanon asked as they traveled on later that morning. "It once was part of your People, yes?"

Forni shook his head. "I don't know for certain," he said. "But the famine…that feels to me as if that was when the land finally turned its back on us, on the Bone People."

"Why did it do that?" Noalanon said.

"I don't know why," Forni said. "There had been some rumors, quickly squashed, that the famine had been caused by the priests, that they'd been trying some great magic and it had failed. Instead of killing their intended victims, bringing their spirits under control, they killed all the lands."

"That's horrible!" Noalanon said. "How could they do that to their own people? Their own land?"

"As I said, no one knows for certain if that's true," Forni added hastily. "If it is true, it was a terrible mistake. Not something that anyone would do on purpose." He gave a visible shudder. "Famine—seeing everyone in a town all starving together—you can't imagine it."

While there were many things that Forni lied about, the famine was not one of them. A haunted look filled his eyes every time he talked of it.

"The people had to eat," Forni continued on. "Had to find food. So they captured all the nearby songbirds, killed off entire species. Chopped down trees to get at the soft, edible bark. Plucked all the grass out of yards to eat the sweet roots. Ate the ants, crickets, grasshoppers. Everything."

He turned his baleful gaze at her. "What we would have given if we could have just eaten minerals, like you. I'm sure some tried eating the dirt. Something. Anything to fill their bellies."

Noalanon just nodded. Famine did indeed sound like a terrible thing. Ze was glad that zir people had never experienced something like that. Never would experience something like that. Zir people would always be able to find enough minerals to live on.

Wouldn't they?

"The winter was the worst," Forni said, looking forward again. "No grass. Nothing green. Just wind and cold and snow. Many gave up completely."

Noalanon wasn't sure what Forni was seeing, but ze knew the sight probably filled his nightmares.

"When spring came and the crops started coming in, I thought that maybe the land hadn't abandoned us. That Valtyr hadn't turned away from us," Forni said. "But nothing ever grew the same. I don't know what caused the famine. That was when the land first turned away from us, though."

Noalanon didn't know what to say. How could one woo one's land back to accepting its People?

And would the invasion of the Bone People cause zir own lands to reject zir People?

NOALANON PULLED on the reins of the cart, stopping the oxen when what appeared to be a guard stepped out onto the road. Killapany was just over the next hill. They hadn't passed by many merchants on the road, which struck Noalanon as strange.

Forni, sitting beside zir, seemed shocked. Of course, he hadn't seen the guard. Ze had been standing perfectly still beside a large stone boulder. The natural camouflage of the Stone People let them blend in, making them hardly noticeable. Nor did he see the other three who stayed in their position.

"What business have you in Killapany?" the guard asked, walking toward them. Ze had a long obsidian knife tucked into zir belt. Ze dropped zir hand to its handle.

This was where it got tricky. The messenger had warned them about the guards on the main roads. Were the guards still under the control of the Bone People? Or had the council broken free, and had the guards been placed there to stop any additional Bone People from coming into the city?

"We come from the land of the Wind People," Noalanon

said. "We bring news." They couldn't pose as merchants, as they had no goods loaded in the back of the cart. And according to the messenger, news was still welcomed, though it would be carefully controlled.

"And who is this?" the guard asked, peering at Forni.

"A Bone Person seeking refuge," Noalanon said.

The guard stared hard at Forni for a few more moments. "No other Bone People with you?" ze asked.

"No, none," Noalanon said. Had the council broken free? Would the guards turn Forni back?

After a long paused, the guard finally nodded and stepped back. "You should take the Bone Person to Valtyr's temple," ze said. "It at the eastern corner of the main market."

"We will," Noalanon promised, feeling an equal mix of both relief and sadness.

The council and the guards were still under the control of the Bone People, as the foreign god's temple was still being built.

But at least ze had been allowed into zir own city. Ze was going to be reunited with Jolapen soon.

Noalanon drove the cart forward, urging the oxen to trot faster.

When they crested the next hill, Noalanon couldn't help but sigh in contentment. This was the city of zir heart. Subtle grays, blacks, browns, and whites made up the buildings, walls, and roofs. It looked like a beautiful mosaic of stone. Ze could already see the pillars that functioned as the northern gate, with lumpy sides and a narrow top, an artist's representation of the holy mountain.

Ze couldn't help the grin ze gave Forni. "Let me show you my city," ze said proudly.

Like most of the other People, he didn't see the beauty right away.

He would learn.

———

FORNI QUICKLY AGREED to be taken to the temple when Noalanon asked.

"While the others will know that I am a freed slave, they won't have any way of finding out that I was helping the Wind People," he reasoned. "I'm still just one of them."

That made sense to Noalanon. Plus, ze had no desire to bring the Bone Person to zir home. Even though, as a teacher, ze had contact with a lot of the other People, very few had ever been invited to zir home. Ka Lem had been the most recent.

Ze still felt badly about Ka Lem. Where was he? And what about Daleki? Were they still in the company of the Bone People? Or had they been freed? Ze wasn't sure that ze would ever find out.

It was obvious to Noalanon that the people in the city were used to seeing Bone People. No one stared at them, not like in the villages they'd passed through.

Ze also saw at least one large group of Bone People walking through the street. It made sense to zir later why they wouldn't travel individually—an angry sSone Person might take out zir rage on a solitary Bone Person. If they traveled in groups and always had a priest with them, the priest might be able to mollify any of the Stone People who decided to take matters into their own hands.

Several of the tea shops and restaurants were closed. That struck Noalanon as strange.

Unless the Bone People were trying to prevent the Stone People from gathering.

Noalanon took the road that skirted the edges of the market. Still, even from there ze could see that many of the stalls were now empty. It was the end of winter. The spring equinox would be upon them shortly. Shouldn't people already be preparing for Kiproary's celebration?

Though Noalanon had missed Killapany, zir city had changed significantly while ze had been gone. It seemed more subdued, the people moving more slowly through the streets.

Finally, they drew around the last corner and approached the temple. Noalanon didn't remember what had once stood there. Some sort of warehouse or storage for the merchants, perhaps.

Now, a graceful compound took over an entire block. The walls were eight feet tall—much higher than the normal, three-feet wall meant to delimitate one family's yard from another. The walls were built from a beautiful, reddish stone that had been formed into blocks and fitted together perfectly, leaving no cracks. Tall buildings rose from behind the wall, built from black stone, or more likely, built from something solid and then faced with black.

Even from the street Noalanon could see the grand tower rising in the center of the temple complex. While there were both two- and three-story buildings in the city, the tower rose above them all.

It was the arrogance of the Bone People, writ large.

Bone People guards stood at the main gate to the temple. They stared hard at Forni. Their pale faces appeared to grow whiter.

Though Noalanon had planned on stopping in the road, the guards grabbed the harnesses of the oxen and pulled them through the gate.

Noalanon quickly looked over at Forni. The smugness of his smile concerned zir.

What was going on? Ze suddenly had a really bad feeling about this.

But it was too late. The oxen pulled the cart forward, into the courtyard of the temple complex.

Suddenly, a mass of Bone People surrounded the cart. The oxen stopped. Forni stood, his arms outstretched, as if he was blessing them all.

Noalanon looked at Hirshamin and Yunaki. They were both shaking their heads.

They'd never trusted Forni. Only Noalanon had taken him at his word.

The gates to the temple closed behind them, locking them in.

More of the Bone People poured out of the nearby buildings. How many were in the city? Noalanon wondered if the messenger hadn't known the truth as they had estimated only two dozen or so. Or had many arrived after the messenger had left Killapany? There were close to fifty that Noalanon could see, possibly more.

"My friends!" Forni said, calling out, his lilting voice sounding happy. "I have returned, as I told you I would!"

Damn it. Noalanon had been fooled. Forni hadn't been a slave, as he'd claimed.

"The Stone People have seen our superiority and brought me here, of their own free will!" Forni continued.

"That's not true," Noalanon said. Ze couldn't help it.

"Do you have your own will?" Forni asked, one eyebrow arching up.

"We do," Noalanon had to admit. "But it had nothing to do with your supposed superiority. We believed you. Felt sorry for you. A slave."

Forni beamed at zir. "Who is a king, but a slave to the people?" he asked softly.

A king?

Noalanon looked on in horror as three priests came out, carrying a rich robe that Forni draped over his shoulders.

The priests kept exclaiming how happy they were now that King Einar had returned to them.

King Einar?

A dark cloud rolled toward the Stone People. They all spiked their internal temperatures, but would it be enough against the collective power of all the priests now surrounding them?

As the darkness washed over zir, Noalanon's last thought was of Jolapen.

____

Chapter Twelve

SEA

AJOOLESS SMELLED the river long before they reached it. It was the largest body of water that they'd passed in some time. Sure, there had been smaller tributaries and the occasional lake. However, there weren't many rivers here.

This had probably been the reason why none of the Sea People had been able to find the home waters of the Bone People.

There weren't any.

Or rather, Ajooless now suspected that what she'd found originally had been an aquifer, deep under the ground of Melefels, the capital of the Bone People.

As Ajooless had been so new to searching, she hadn't been looking specifically for rivers or lakes, just for *water*. This was why no one had been able to follow what she'd found. The others weren't looking deep enough.

It was yet one more thing that Ajooless committed to memory, the long report that she'd make if she were ever allowed to return home.

In the meanwhile, she rested in the back of one of the Bone People's carts. They'd tried attaching iron shackles and a chain to her ankles, but the pain and cold of the iron had made Ajooless scream for hours. She couldn't help herself. Whatever magic had been woven into the iron pained her very soul. She couldn't tolerate it. None of the Sea People would be able to, she suspected.

So instead, they kept her tied with ropes to the end of the cart. She never tried to escape. It was her duty to see this through to the end, to figure out what the Bone People really, truly were up to.

Only then would she do everything in her power to leave.

She'd already formed more than one plan that might work. Because she'd been so acquiescent, the Bone People had gotten sloppy around her. Hopefully it wouldn't be that difficult to escape when the time came.

They drew closer to the river. They didn't think to watch her more carefully as they crossed over a wide bridge. They didn't know how much the waters called to her.

Or how much she learned about the Bone People just by being so near to a large body of water.

It appeared that this river was originally a border. In many ways, it was the true edge of the Bone People's land, which actually lay to the west of here. They'd been traveling through land claimed by the Bone People for several days, but it wasn't theirs. Not really.

The river grew mightier both to the north and south of this point—the road was here because this was where the river was the narrowest and the most tame.

Boats with colorful sails traversed the river. Ajooless could taste the well-made craft, the slick sides. The people who sailed them were almost a different People than the Bone People, a River People who, in some ways, more resembled her own folk, as they were so tied to the water.

Had there been yet a fifth People at one point? One

whom the Bone People had already assimilated? It had happened centuries before, if at all. But it might also explain why the Bone People were good with water, if they'd mingled with the River People.

It surprised Ajooless when the cart suddenly turned north, traveling beside the river. The city didn't lie that way. It had been straight ahead.

It took her just a moment to trace the water from the main river up.

There was a tributary up here whose waters tasted very different. The water itself was thicker, and it carried a strange power.

Ajooless didn't allow herself to smile when the cart turned and started following along the path of the smaller tributary.

They passed under a large white arch, decorated in bones. They reminded her of the arches over the piers that led into the water from Sillboden.

The Bone People had proclaimed these waters to be deadly. Did they not understand the power? Or was it merely deadly to them?

Ajooless sat, waiting with great anticipation when the carts came to a halt. She sent her water sense out to the tributary. The power there lay pooled, waiting to be tapped. If only she could reach it…

She heard Helge the priest chanting, asking for the blessing of the abyss, the protection of bone. It seemed odd to her that he wasn't calling on the power of the water that was right there, beside him.

Did he not feel it? The Bone People recognized that the river wasn't to be trifled with, given the arch they'd passed through. Did they merely fear the water?

When two guards came into her line of view, she nearly

gasped. They were outlined in a blue glow, a shield of some sort. Whatever did they need that protection for?

They carried a large barrel that had been cut in half between them. Rigidly, they approached the water.

So the Bone People did understand that the water wasn't safe. The priest had put up some sort of protection for the guards, so the water couldn't touch them.

Why were they then gathering a barrel of water? What would they do with it?

Ajooless couldn't have been more surprised when the guards approached her, then dumped it on her.

And Ajooless dreamed.

***

WHEN AJOOLESS CAME BACK to herself, the cart was still at rest. Helge stood beside her, his face white and pinched with anger.

"What did you see?" he demanded.

"Nothing," Ajooless immediately lied. She gasped at the air, filling her lungs, trying to come fully back to her land self. She hadn't transformed into her sea form, not even with that water. Still, it had carried her away, taken her outside of herself. She sat up, her head still dizzy and full of dreams.

"You saw something," Helge said. He shook his head. "I told the others that bringing one of your kind here was the worst thing we could do." He spat toward the river. "I would compel you to speak, if I could."

Ajooless cocked her head to one side. "Why don't you?" It had been a few weeks since she'd had to suffer any of Helge's sermons, have her land form controlled until the next time she could touch water.

"It would ruin the ceremony," he said. He gave her a

baleful grin. "Just you wait. Then you will know our true power."

"And not just the power you've taken from other People?" Ajooless said, taunting him.

Helge's entire body stiffened. In fear? Or so that he wouldn't reach out and hit her?

"What did you see?" he asked again.

"Your beginnings," she told him, only exaggerating a little. "And your end."

"Bah!" Helge said, stomping away to the cart that bore him, somewhere in front of her, out of her line of vision.

The cart bearing Ajooless jerked forward. Ajooless sat up, cradling the boost of power that had come from the river, deep in her belly.

She had finally learned enough.

It was time for her to escape.

UNFORTUNATELY, since the encounter at the river, Ajooless' guards were more attentive. She still had more strength than she'd had earlier, so it would be just a matter of time, a single slip-up.

Then, she'd be gone. Melted away like morning fog.

They were closer to the main city now, she could tell. They passed through larger and larger villages. People stared at her. They crossed their arms over their chest when they saw her, as if to protect themselves from her very presence.

She saw the evidence of the famine everywhere. Holes where trees or a park might have once stood. Dirty yards where once grass had grown, only to be plucked short by a hungry people pulling up the shoots and eating them. No flowers to brighten the soul, or even bright colored clothing.

No life outside of their own existence, except for the black abyss of their god.

It pained Ajooless to see any people suffer so.

She'd seen how the Bone People had been born among the mountain ranges far to the east of where they now called home. They'd been peaceful at first, trading with the River People who lived on all the rivers and lakes in the center region. They'd even been able to inter-marry, something that surprised Ajooless, as none of the remaining Peoples could even consider breeding together.

The buildup to hostilities between the two People had been so gradual, and certainly not one-sided. The wars between them had been so terrible that the Wind, Stone, and Sea Peoples had eventually gotten involved, sending healers and aid but not warriors. The stories got lost though, or turned into myths.

The River People were eventually defeated, and either lived among the Bone People as second-class citizens, or worked as slaves.

Ajooless had never seen such a terrible place before as a mine. While it might have been natural to the Stone People, it was completely alien to the River People. They died young and heartbroken, and needed to be replaced often.

But the Bone People needed their metal, needed the horrible coal they burned in their cities instead of wood.

The plains were clear, the breezes blowing cleanly across them. But back in the east, closer to the mountains, there were terrible cities, terrible places, where the air was unclean and the land stripped of its life. Only the poorest lived there, almost unrecognizable compared to the people Ajooless saw around her.

The famine had been caused by their own people. They'd pulled so much magic out of the very earth itself that it could no longer sustain itself, or the people living on it.

And now…Ajooless feared what they planned now. The waters had shown her how the priests had banded together, then stolen the souls of a curious creature called a horse, and now the elk.

The waters had told Ajooless of Ka Lem, how they'd tasted him a short while ago, a people they were unfamiliar with. And now, they'd tasted her as well.

Would the priests try to take the entire soul of the Wind People? And the Sea People? Possibly the Stone People as well, though the waters were uncertain about whether they'd tasted one like that.

She wasn't about to wait and find out. She'd learned how to follow the waters back here from the sea, how to identify the little tributary of power, how the Sea People could cause an even worse plague and hold back the Bone People.

It would take years for the full effects to be known. But Ajooless had the key now.

The Sea People didn't have to poison the Bone People. They were actually killing themselves off, those of true blood, by using so much magic. Instead of relying on themselves for power, they constantly sipped it off of their surroundings. It had made them very strong, but very weak at the same time. Their lands were no longer bountiful as the Bone People depleted the magic they'd once contained.

They needed to invade the lands of the Wind, Stone, and Sea Peoples in order to refresh their magic and make themselves strong again, never considering what would happen once they ran out of land to consume.

Isolating them would go far in terms of weakening them.

In addition, the Sea People could make the Bone People sterile.

Only those with enough mixed blood would be able to have offspring. And the River People didn't have an affinity toward the abyss, not like the Bone People did. The priest's terrible magic would fade, and the River People would return to the water, away from the darkness.

Some of the Bone People might survive, but their power would be greatly muted.

She just had to get home, or else have a message carried there.

But how?

THE CITY of Melefels held no surprises for Ajooless. She'd already seen it clearly, seen how stripped bare the land had become, how rusted and pitted some of the once-graceful metal sculptures were now, how hungry the people were, even with more food available.

Streets wound around on themselves, set in concentric circles around the center hub. Spokes ran out from there in straight lines, bisecting the neighborhoods. Each group of the Bone People had their place, where they were born, lived, and died. The society was very stratified, even more so than the Sea People's.

She knew, though, that the underlying reason for this structure was to power the priests. They could draw on the strength of all the people when they performed their great magics only because the people were not mixed in the cities, or in the camps—the exact placement of their people enabled the priests to tap the exact type and amount from each group.

As when they'd taken the horses, and then the elk.

Ajooless saw her opportunity after they'd reached their final destination. She assumed that the area had at one point been a large market. Now, the priests had confiscated it, using it for their ceremonies.

She was finally released from the cart and allowed to

walk, what little she could. She'd lost a tremendous amount of strength from not being able to move on her own. She pretended, however, to be as weak as a minnow.

The guards relaxed their vigilance around her even more than they had previously. They probably assumed that since there were no bodies of water nearby, that she couldn't escape. There was nowhere for her to run.

They'd forgotten the well, located less than one hundred feet from the tent they'd enclosed her in. The cart had passed by it on their way in, and Ajooless could still feel it.

A large stone oval, nearly five feet across, stood at the top of the deep hole. It had two bucket draws so that more than one person could use it at the same time. At one point, it had probably been very active, with merchants drawing water from it all day long.

The well was fed by a deep underground river, as well as the aquifer. She knew if she could just get to the water, she could escape. She wouldn't have to surface until the first large river they'd crossed days ago.

She just had to bide her time, until the guards were distracted, so that she could escape. At night, Ajooless stretched and tried to strengthen her legs by squatting on them, holding up her weight. It wasn't much, but she had to be able to run quickly to the well at a moment's notice.

The guards seemed very excited one evening, as if the next day would be a huge celebration. She asked what was going on, but they ignored her, as always.

Ajooless had heard them arguing amongst themselves more than once how she couldn't be a person because she didn't look like one. Some of them even seemed startled when she spoke. None of the Bone People tried to befriend her.

While she missed having people to talk with, Ajooless told herself that it was just part of her training, to become a high priestess. Her own people held her at arm's length. This separateness was always going to be part of her life.

But it made more sense to her now why Liseth had made every effort to befriend her younger acolyte. The priestesses needed to rely on each other.

The tent that held Ajooless was made out of a dull, thick cloth that baked during the day and didn't let any breezes in. Fortunately, she could handle the stifling heat, better than the Bone People, and so was frequently left on her own for most of the day. They've given her a nicer bedroll, as well as a much better robe than she'd had before. She didn't have enough water to bathe her dry and cracking skin, though she tried to wash at least her arms every day.

The day dawned hot and still. Ajooless knew, though, that it was still spring. The real heat wouldn't arrive for a few months, when it would be unbearable.

And yet the Bone People covered all their skin. All the time.

Outside, Ajooless heard drums beating. Loud flutes wailed. The cadence of a chant rolled underneath the noise.

The priests were starting a ceremony. Something big and important, she'd bet.

However, it had nothing to do with her. They would have come to prepare her if she was to be part of it.

No, this was for something else.

Or someone else.

Ajooless poked her head out of the tent. The guards stood at rigid attention.

No, not that.

They were in a trance. The priests had already tapped into the power of those nearby.

Ajooless paused for a moment. They weren't able to reach her, or her People.

Good to know.

She looked at the guards again, waiting until their eyes were turned completely inward.

They were blind to everything happening outside of themselves.

It was time for her escape.

Quickly, Ajooless scurried out of the tent, heading directly for the well as fast as her sore feet would carry her.

She saw it just ahead of her. Just a few more feet.

"Stop!" someone from behind her called.

Ajooless put on a burst of speed. She could do this. She could make it.

She could escape.

She didn't slow down until she reached the tall wall surrounding the well. She placed her hands on the top and brought herself up to the lip.

She didn't know why she turned back at that moment. But she did.

Ka Lem hung from a tree, dazed. He wore a robe similar to hers.

Priests passed by him. Priests with knives. Priests who cut him with every pass.

"Stop!!!"

Ajooless could wait no longer, and dove into the deep dark well, splashing into the welcoming water at the bottom, knowing she was already too late.

MYTHS OF THE THIRD AGE

The Wind People's Creation Myth

IN THE BEGINNING, Sune Li danced alone in the dark. He/She decided to create companions and gave birth to Gan Zhur and Ban Zhur, the first two people. They asked for solid earth beneath their feet so that they could better dance for the God/Goddess. Sune Li called Kiproary out of the darkness, so that he/she could form the world. Kiproary called Ishkra out of the firmament, so that she could bring the forgetting rains and the waters of rebirth.

Sune Li set his/her lively spark deep in the heart of all living things, so that they might learn their true self and dance always in his/her light.

THE GOD/GODDESS of the Wind People goes by many names. Sune Li, God/Goddess of the flame/light is most common. But frequently the God/Goddess is called

Nameless One, the One God, the Lively One, Bringer of Light and Life.

Sune Li is not represented by any particular form, not embodied in any one creature. The God/Goddess may be represented by a carving of a flame, or a single candle, though in older times, was represented by a circle with radiating lines, representing the sun. But Sune Li is found in all light, not just sunlight.

As a soul ages, one of the goals for a Wind Person is to take every animal shape known, so as to be closer to Sune Li and achieve their own enlightenment, to move beyond physical form so they can just be a spirit, endless as a wind.

The Stone People's Creation Myth

Kiproary drifted in the darkness, a towering mountain in the blackness that existed before the stars. Ze awoke slowly, peering through the abyss and finding none to stare back. Kiproary looked behind Zir and started leaving a trail of bright lights for other to follow, once they took shape themselves. After many adventures, Kiproary decided to settle down. Ze formed the earth around Zir, setting Zir strength down into the core of the world, declaring this place and all the lands as sacred to Zir.

Kiproary created others like Zirself, tall and proud people who took to the firmament to grow. However, they were too static. They didn't move like the animals, but were more like the mountains. Kiproary found that while Ze could move around the stars, Zir people needed help to move on the earth.

So Kiproary invited Sune Li to follow Zir to the earth, to give all creatures movement. The people grew proud. To keep them humble, Kiproary also invited Ishkra and the waters of death and rebirth, as a reminder that the smallest trickle could cut a channel into stone over time, that even the tallest mountain could be reduced into pebbles eventually.

KIPROARY IS MOST OFTEN REPRESENTED by a drawing of a rounded hill. A sharp peak is considered ignorant, or arrogant, or both. Just a pebble placed on a table can sanctify a location. As well as sprinkling dirt finely ground from the holy mountain, where Kiproary first stepped down and walked the firmament.

The Sea People's Creation Myth

Ishkra floated with her siblings through the darkness until they formed the world, each placing their essence into the firmament so that life could begin.

The first people Ishkra birthed had no magic. They were solid as the mountains and as lively as the winds. But they were arrogant. They considered themselves the masters of all, and didn't respect the lives or light of others. They burned the forests, polluted the waters, carved the mountains into little pieces. And they warred with one another constantly, until finally, with the help of the gods, they destroyed themselves utterly. Thus ended the Age of Greed.

The second people Ishkra birthed were strictly a sea people. The waters were wide and plentiful, and the sea people had to live in harmony with their environment, learning quickly that they were dependent on the world and the waters.

But there were too many of them. Ishkra had favored them with multiple births, and they quickly ran out of space. They couldn't survive out of the water, and the gods turned their faces away from those who tried.

Diseases began to run rampant. Even their magic couldn't save them. Eventually, with the help of the gods, the people all died out. Thus ended the Age of the Sea.

The third people Ishkra birthed knew both land and sea. She let first Kiproary, then Sune Li, touch her pregnant belly, so that the Stone and Wind Peoples would be born as well. The Peoples were different, so they would live different lives in separate places. They all had magic, so they would see each other as equals. And they were all lively, so that they could dance and worship the gods.

Ishkra takes all souls and washes them clean at death, giving them another chance to live a pious life. The gods watch and wait, lest the people forget themselves, and decide to challenge the gods. If they do, the world will end in fire and all the Peoples, with the help of the gods, will die. Then the current age, the Third Age, will end.

ISHKRA IS REPRESENTED by a wavy line. Pure water will sanctify a space. Myths revolve around sincerely holy people who can do it through merely spitting. Knowledge and learning are valued above all. The Sea People have many more regular prayers during the day. Leading a pious life is more important to them than any of the other Peoples.

The Bone People's Creation Myth

Valtyr swam through his home, reveling in the absolute darkness. He needed no light, no firm ground, no water to bring him life. The abyss was everything. He needed nothing more.

Still, sometimes Valtyr was lonely. So He allowed others to form in the darkness: Sune Li, Kiproary, and Ishkra. But they didn't celebrate the darkness as He did. They disrespected their home, as well as the being who had allowed them to be born. They celebrated their own individual natures first and foremost, instead of relishing the dark like Valtyr did, or muchless respecting it and giving the abyss its well-deserved prayers.

So Valtyr banished them, sending them out of the darkness and onto the other side, away from the firmament and into the ether.

Occasionally, word of the others traveled across the abyss to Valtyr. It made Him happy to see His children thrive, though none of them acknowledged Him or His place as the greatest of all the gods.

But the Bone People, those who initially stayed behind with Valtyr in the darkness, learned the truth. They knew of the power of the abyss, the true power of death.

Eventually, after many adventures, the Bone People traveled from the abyss into the light, learned to live on the ground instead of swimming between the stars. Valtyr allowed them to be bathed in the waters of forgetfulness between births, though He forbade them to dance as the other Peoples.

The Bone People worshipped Valtyr every waking hour, knowing the absolute power of death over life, relishing the abyss and the dark places.

Valtyr heard the prayers of the other People, of the Wind and Stone and Sea People. Heard their boastfulness, heard their celebrations of light. Finally, He had had enough.

He sent great leaders to the Bone People, powerful leaders who could show them the way, to teach them to use the deaths of others to strengthen themselves.

Now, the Bone People have been called to right the wrongs paid to Valtyr, to show the other Peoples the error of their ways, to bring them all home to the darkness, to swim once again in the waters of the abyss.

Or to bring them death if they refuse.

VALTYR IS REPRESENTED by any sort of bone, though just a line across the dirt will do. All important prayers are done inside, in the dark. Dancing can be punished by death.

About the Author

Leah Cutter writes page-turning fiction in exotic locations, such as a magical New Orleans, the ancient Orient, Hungary, the Oregon coast, rural Kentucky, Seattle, Minneapolis, and many others.

She writes literary, fantasy, mystery, science fiction, and horror fiction. Her short fiction has been published in magazines like *Alfred Hitchcock's Mystery Magazine* and *Talebones*, anthologies like Fiction River, and on the web. Her long fiction has been published both by New York publishers as well as small presses.

Find Leah's books on Knotted Road Press at (www.KnottedRoadPress.com)

Follow her blog at www.LeahCutter.com.

Reviews

It's true. Reviews help me sell more books. If you've enjoyed this story, please consider leaving a review of it on your favorite site.

Come someplace new…

Are you a traveler? Do you enjoy exploring strange new worlds, new cultures, new people?

Journey into the various lands envisioned by Leah Cutter.

Sign up for my newsletter and I'll start you on your travels with a free copy of my book, *The Island Sampler*.

I will never spam you or use your email for nefarious purposes. You can also unsubscribe at any time.

http://www.LeahCutter.com/newsletter/

About Knotted Road Press

Knotted Road Press fiction specializes in dynamic writing set in mysterious, exotic locations.

Knotted Road Press non-fiction publishes autobiographies, business books, cookbooks, and how-to books with unique voices.

Knotted Road Press creates DRM-free ebooks as well as high-quality print books for readers around the world.

With authors in a variety of genres including literary, poetry, mystery, fantasy, and science fiction, Knotted Road Press has something for everyone.

Knotted Road Press
www.KnottedRoadPress.com